Helen.

Helen.

Oswald Valentine Sickert

With an Editorial Note by Denis Boyles

Managing Editor, *Fortnightly Review*, etc.

ODD VOLUMES

OF

THE FORTNIGHTLY REVIEW

LES BROUZILS 2014

ISBN: 978-0692296172

Odd Volumes Edition.

AUTHOR'S DEDICATION

To Edward Marsh.

TABLE OF CONTENTS

INTRODUCTION

THE FORTNIGHTLY REVIEW's 2013 serial was *Helen*, by Oswald Valentine Sickert. It had originally been published in 1894 as number 44 in T. Fisher Unwin's "Pseudonym Library" series. (Sickert's "pseudonym" was simply "Oswald Valentine".) Sickert's study of late Victorian characters reveals not only something of its time but especially the social setting of the man who wrote it.

 Oswald's book is a slight and delicate work, much like Oswald himself. In *Helen*, two characters – George, an ambitious writer and a freshly liberated woman, Helen – and the quite modern, upper-middle-class relationship they maintained are revealed in elaborate detail.

Sickert was a very timid author. The manuscript for *Helen* was shown by him to many of those whom he thought might help improve it, including, even, Frank Harris. Edward Marsh, a Cambridge friend who gave the book an edit before publication, recalled in 1939, "[Oswald] wrote with infinite pains and utter integrity a novel...but nobody read it. Such fire as he had was banked under his 'artistic conscience'; he kept his tone so perfectly that nothing stood out; he was so careful not to say too much that he seemed to be saying nothing at all."

He did speak softly, perhaps, but he was not a man without views—especially on art and politics, both of which are lampooned in *Helen*, which is a rather autobiographical book mirroring Oswald's own negotiations with society and the great movements of the day. Like Oswald, his confused protagonist, George, finds little comfort in these.

Sickert, born on Valentine's Day 1871,[1] was the younger brother of painter Walter Sickert, who was ten years older, and, like virtually every other writer and artist in London, an acquaintance of James McNeill Whistler's, under whom Walter had worked and studied and suffered. Whistler's vast network of friends and former-friends-turned-adversaries, such as Walter and Oswald Sickert, composed an interwoven wreath of accomplished, thin-skinned people all of whom knew each other perhaps a bit too well; Sickert's family was especially absorbed in the artistic skirmishes of the day. No wonder George issues a straightforward, if temporary, rebuke of "art" — which he sees as an ineffectual, trivial pastime, compared to the day's social issues:

> Art could not mean a full occupation, an energetic life to such as they: it had been, and it would be; but it was not then. Social questions, in the broadest sense, were now the fit study of the young generation.

But for George, as apparently for Oswald, Socialism, too, was a false refuge. He and Helen both try to live their lives in obedience to what Helen calls "their divine gospel...the cause of humanity." In the end, they are left dissatisfied and as distracted by the Socialist obsessions of their friends as any anxious "intellectual" would be today. At one point, George is astonished to discover that he has become "that sort of person, a 'Sozial-Kopf'," when all along he had been considering himself to be an artist.

The Sickert family was indeed a complicated little troupe. The father, Oswald Adalbert, a melancholy Danish-born painter, and his wife, Nelly (Eleanor), produced five boys – only two of whom were ultimately unemployable, although one of them

– Leonard, also called Leo – nearly made a living as a singer. Walter was the famous painter, and a daughter, Helena, the suffragist. Oswald was by far the most conventional Sickert.[2]

At the time *Helen* was written, the family had long made a second home in Dieppe, where Walter painted on the beach while his brothers walked along the shore or spent slow afternoons under the long arcade facing the harbor. In an 1895 letter to his Cambridge friend, Edward Marsh, Oswald Sickert sketched his own, somewhat rosy, view of family life far from the gloom he had found at Cambridge:

> 'I often wonder whether you would like this place: on the whole, I think you would, though I know now that the Sickerts can't expect other people to see in Dieppe all that it means to them… I suppose I was about seven when I first came, in the spring-time: I stayed with my sister at Mother's old school, and the girls and I used to make houses with bricks and twigs and carpet them with the petals of peonies. Then a little later the school stopped and we took the house for the summer, and I remember Oscar [Wilde] reading us his poems in the meadow in front of the house, and playing with Leo and me. Once, when he was reading his poems dear old Miss Slea, the schoolmistress, 'Aunty' we used to call her, interrupted him and said: 'No, my dear fellow, not like that: now begin again.' Johnston Forbes-Robertson [the great actor] was with us too, but I can't recall him…Then one day Whistler arrived, and he used to be at odd corners, standing upright, immaculate, dainty, doing little water-colours as another man would roll a cigarette; and then Degas came too, and I shall never forget the gentleness and the charm of his personality. That was all very long ago, and I don't feel as if I lived a separate existence then.'[3]

Oswald learned to dance and, under the tutelage of his brother, Leo, "made a speciality of clapping the right people" and sitting on the casino ballroom window sills "to listen to the adored Rivard playing the violin." Literary and artistic friends would come and go:

'[Last] year, when Stanley [Makower] was here, we had the best time of all, and on ball-nights Leo would come and laugh with us between the dances; then we sent him on to the café first, and we followed when the dance was over and sat drinking Loewenbräu. That's the Café de Rouen, to the side of the Café des Tribunaux, and it was there that when I was here alone Walter always used to meet met at 12.30 and draw pictures on the little round tables, and catch sight of his famous Madame de Something, driving her pair of spanking greys about at midnight with white kid gloves on. There can never be any other place for me quite like this.'[4]

Sickert, according to his sister, the feminist writer and editor Helena Maria Swanwick, was simply "much the best of us all....even as a young man he had much the better and more considerate manners than any that I knew." Others, especially Janet (Hogarth) Courtney, his colleague at the Times Book Club, enjoyed his soothing gentility, agreeing, no doubt, with his sister who found that "he was impossible to anticipate, because he was authentic and because his mind was uncommonly discriminating. His attitude to life had something religious about it: he reverenced and savoured not only people but materials and emotions, so that he was fastidiously temperate and capable of ecstasy" – if not of hard work.

"He was a terrible worker," his sister admitted, "and he used to excuse himself by saying that he had to be, because he was slow," not in his thinking, but in his preferred manner. He once told her that his idea of a perfect vacation "was to do what he usually did, but [to take]ten times as long in doing it." Once, explaining to a doubtful Helena how to properly enjoy buckwheat porridge, one of his favorite dishes (and one of her least), he said, "Ah you haven't found the technique of *Buchwaizen*. It is faint, at *first*. But if you wait for a minute or two after you've eaten a spoonful, the most heavenly ghost of a taste appears. Almost as heavenly as the best smells." Helena pointed out that eating breakfast that slowly would take all morning. "But I thought we were talking about a *taste!*" Oswald scolded, "Not about being in time for the office."[5] As with buckwheat porridge, so, for some, with Sickert's fiction.

OSWALD ATTENDED CAMBRIDGE where he helped launch a weekly newspaper, the *Cambridge Observer*, chummed with Bertrand Russell (who read several of Oswald's first stories, as well as the manuscript for this book), pursued women chastely and socialized on the margins of the Apostles, although he was never a member. His best friends were Russell, Lowes Dickinson, the composer Dalhousie Young, Eddie Marsh and especially Roger Fry, who became a close friend of the Sickert family, with whom he found companionship and lodging when his wife became mentally unstable. Fry called Oswald "the most entirely beautiful character I have ever known."[6]

The paper, The *Cambridge Observer*, was a project by Oswald and a few friends – identified by Russell, who was one of them, as "a clique of high-brow and extremely literary Cambridge undergraduates."[7] Oswald gave Russell his first appearance in print. In 1893, a trio of Observer editors, Oswald, Stanley Makower and Arthur Myers Smith, collaborated on *The Passing of a Mood*, number 30 in the Pseudonym Library (and in which an early rehearsal of "Helen" appeared). Both Makower and Sickert appeared in the list of contributors to *The Yellow Book* in 1894, the year Oswald's *Helen*, published under the name Oswald Valentine, finally appeared.

"This sensitive and exquisite creature," to use Marsh's description, joined the reviewing staff of the *Saturday Review*, and from there was recruited by the proprietor of the *Encyclopædia Britannica*, first to help run The Times Book Club on Oxford Street, and then to head the *Britannica's* controversial and prolific advertising department. Soon, he was circling the globe. In 1904, when he returned from one of his lengthy voyages, he devoted himself to helping his brother Bernard, a nearly incapacitated alcoholic with pretensions to a writing and artistic career, like his brother, Walter. His sister thought it preposterous that he should touch down in the Orient and India, in the U.S., in southern and central Africa – "even in Spain," which is where he was when he unexpectedly died in 1923, leaving behind a widow, an actress named Elizabeth Kennedy.

Sickert, as Marsh recalled, had "spent years of his life as a 'traveler' in the Dominions for the new edition of the *Encyclopædia Britannica*," often delegated to survey the Asian and Imperial markets for the set. These had mixed results: after one sales journey to China and Japan, he contributed a very thoughtful and well- researched collection of letters that eventually were published in Arthur Waley's *Nō Plays of Japan*.[8]

The idea of Sickert finding success in the ad department of the Britannica, the source for many years of some of the most aggressive and hyperbolic advertising of the day, amused those who knew Sickert well. In his situation with the Book Club, he proved to be a lively, gregarious collaborator who worked hard, even as he turned what his sister said a friend called "the finest monosyllabic style in Cambridge" to the Britannica's notorious use of avalanche-language in ad copy, made maddeningly famous by his mentor, H.R. Haxton, a bohemian adman and yet another friend of Whistler's. "It was one of the oddest appointments and oddest successes which I have known," his sister recalled.[9]

— *Denis Boyles*

Les Brouzils 2014.

NOTES.

1. Troy Bassett, victorianresearch.org.

2. Walter Sickert: A Life (2005), by Matthew Sturgis, is a very thorough biography of Walter and provides a detailed and helpful family portrait.

3. Marsh, Edward. A Number of People: A book of reminiscences. Heinemann, London 1939. pp 50-51. Our photographic portrait is from Marsh's book.

4. Ibid.

5. Helena Maria Swanwick, I Have Been Young (London 1935), pp. 350-51.

6. Letters of Roger Fry, edited by Denys Sutton. London 1972. Vol. 2, pp 546-7.

7. Spadoni, Carl "The Curious Case of The Cambridge Observer," Russell: the Journal of Bertrand Russell Studies: Vol. 2: No. 1, Article 12. (1982) Online at: http://digitalcommons.mcmaster.ca/russelljournal/vol2/iss1/12 . Retrieved 12 July 2013.

8. London, 1921, pp 306-316.

9. Swanwick, p. 352.

HELEN.

I.

GEORGE had just left Cambridge. He had grown more and more discontented as his three years drew to an end, as the romances which has been the continual and secret delight of his boyhood became more and more threadbare. As far back as he could remember he had invented romances to please himself, with vague misgivings even at the beginning; but they had continued to occupy his mind. Now they had become uninteresting or hateful, and he was left without the engrossing occupation of his intimate life. He enjoyed his friendships, he had great enthusiasms, he did some work; but he was for ever coming back upon himself to find only bits of old dreams and a causeless melancholy. Not that this indescribable discontent spoilt his pleasure; only it was always there, at the back of everything else, the one thing of which he was sure. Everything else was on the outside and not engrossing enough to touch him intimately. The one reality which he must always face, in spite of all interests, was this spectre of himself.

He was sure now that his early misgivings had been right. If he had not filled his mind so greedily with pleasant dreams all through his boyhood, perhaps now he would not have been left with such a big blank.

One day, wearied out with wondering how it was that, with his strongest efforts, he could not arrive at anything more comforting than an occasional laugh at himself (and it was a great discovery when he found that at moments he could laugh), he said in jest, "I evidently want a religion." The hackneyed words stuck in his mind, and however broad a construction he put on them, he still felt ashamed and disgusted that they should be applicable to him.

He had been independent, he had felt strongly the emancipated young man's objection to admitting any of the recognised laws of morality. And even if he agreed with them, he shrank from using the orthodox phraseology. Thus he naturally resented a falling back upon well-known words, a statement which had been preached to him long before he understood what it could mean. He had always revolted from the teaching of mothers and fathers and schoolmasters, however true it may have been, because there was nothing to appeal to him in the way in which it was expressed. When he was a child he had been delighted to hear a grown man scoffing at the idea that a religion was necessary. He had clung blindly to his literary enthusiasms, just as he had clung to his belief that Cambridge did not suit him, and his hope that when he started upon life he would be easier and less self-centred than in his surroundings at the University. His chief friend, Henry Bishop, joined somewhat cheerfully in George's discontent, Cambridge was certainly not an inspiring place, and he talked about life—life in the world. George talked less; but comforted himself when he could with his vague hopes. He was working at classics for his Tripos, there was no need to be precise; he could write a little now and then, take great pleasure in making favourite novels and plays his own possession, and look forward still more vaguely to—well, he would have been shy of owning it; he only took every occasion in discussion with his friends to defend and idolise women, to declaim against everything that led them out of sympathy with men, and to confess that he loved everything that brought them together—even afternoon calls. That was part of his faith, and he would not be shaken by any doubts, whether they arose from himself or from books and friends. Of his dreams the sweetest and brightest were the moments when his mind was filled with the expectation of success in life, mingled somehow with love; but they did not last long, and would be followed by hours of idle depression, or an emptiness which he felt painfully even through the laughter and conversation in which he took part. Then he felt as if he were at sea and rudderless.

When the boy left Cambridge he had time to look more closely into his hopes; there was no longer any excuse for vagueness. He turned over the scraps of paper on which had written at Cambridge, and earlier still at school the cherished foundation of his hopes, and they showed so little promise, their childishness made him so ashamed, that he was shocked by his own fatuousness in thinking that anything could some from such productions. And the first serious attempts at writing which he made now that has leisure so overwhelmed him with a sense of his incapacity that the first two months of freedom were darkened by the horrible disillusion.

He was to be helped on to an evening paper in August when some of the regular staff would be away, and he had hoped that he might by that time have his vague expectations turned into a certainty. The work which was to be done on the paper would not be very amusing, he had allowed; but he might have time to write now and then—and most certainly he would always have work of his own which he would carry on for his own pleasure. He would come home in the afternoon looking forward to this private work; there would always be something to think over, a centre for his enthusiasm and diligence, a cure for the emptiness and causeless melancholy which had been so heavy till then. But now, when had he to look forward to?

Also he entered upon "life," and there was nothing peculiarly interesting in it. He even found an elegant and charming girl staying at his home; but that did not make much difference. After various conversations with her about their friends and Ibsen's plays, like other conversations not at all exciting, he recognised that this was exactly that great thing to which he had been looking forward. Women's society, then, meant nothing in itself. The destruction of his two hopes at the first trial sent him to the extreme of bitterness.

At moments he saw that he was ridiculous. The world was evidently possible, for look at all the people who were living contentedly; but that thought did not console him, nor, because he had enjoyed himself for an hour or a day, could he feel any lasting foundation of comfort.

A young man is a difficult thing to handle, and very few people think it worth while to try. When his mother saw any little piece of groundless melancholy and boredom, she generally put him off by saying, "Rubbish, my boy; you want something to keep you occupied. You have no real troubles. You eat and sleep all right: it's only idleness." This is one of the truths which are not good to say. It was no comfort to George, and it was put in a way which roused his hostility to everything which older people said, everything together. So instead of answering properly, "Then go and give me something to occupy me," he answered in a spirit of opposition that it was not so at all.

II.

TOWARDS the end of July George was left alone in the house. He went to his work early in the morning, and was generally free soon after four o'clock. He thought he felt better now that he had entirely thrown over the hope of being able to write. It had been of no service, so he would not let it hamper him. He was absolutely empty, like the man in the parable. It was better than worrying. He tried to keep himself as blank as possible. But his mind was active, and he had nothing to occupy his thoughts, so he could not help thinking of himself, inventing love-romances again till he made himself sick, building castles in Spain till he was ashamed of being still such a child, especially when he had already looked a little at life and found that it did not correspond at all with his hopes. He wondered how other people filled their thoughts. And like a man in bed, wishing to sleep, he kept his mind from thinking—he might almost have taken to counting in his endeavour to remain blank.

There must have been something peculiarly wrong, it seemed to him, about his character during June and the beginning of July, to make that period leave such a disagreeable impression on his mind. There was one particular struggle during that time, a source of utter weariness, which he remembered with a shudder. It was an attempt to explain in a story one of the ideas which had vaguely interesting him. A teacher comes as a lecturer to a college school in London. He has a slight personal acquaintance with Taine and Renan, he is enthusiastic, with an interesting, somewhat bohemian, manner. Pupils and parents are delighted with him. When the pupils who have left school see him again, they find him just the same, still enthusiastic, still talking of Taine, still with the same mannerisms. He seems so far back and narrow; but he has others under him who in their turn are caught by his enthusiasm.

For some days he thought only of this: he would not let his mind romance to please himself, he would occupy himself with this idea. Then he tried to express it. First he described the state of things; but that was too explanatory: then he thought a long story could be woven round the theme; but he had not enought knowledge: then he wrote the thing from the point of view of a pupil; but that would not do. He was determined to make this an interest, a complete interest; it was this which should prevent his falling back into the old emptiness; but the struggle was hopeless.

Then came a period of nausea, an empty retching of the disgusted intellect—he had demanded so much.

And finally he became wildly angry. Why should be torture himself over this idiocy? What did he care about theories of expression? He wanted to be out, dancing, taking ladies down the river, enjoying himself in act, in actual life. Art was not the business of a young man; it was a pretty substitute, not fit for him at any rate. But, then, what was there to think about? How did other people fill their thoughts? And so he had reached the blank stage. It was no good doing anything. Either all life was like this, and then he had better resign himself; or else it was better than this; but the improvement must come from outside, if it was to come. He was incapable of moving, because he had no ground to walk on—he could not look at anything for space was empty.

A new source of annoyance had come upon him; another of those strange unheard-of things. All his little personal habits pushed themselves into view. Instead of passing unnoticed as the inevitable details of existence, his little peculiarities forced their way into notice, and then grew heavy and formed a great chain of weights which stretched over the day. Suppose he told any one of this? He imagined himself giving an example. No;

people would either think that he was mad, or wished to think that he was mad, or wished to be interesting and modern. Or if anybody saw the truth, they would be disgusted, as he was.

One hot morning just before lunch George was walking home past Kensington Church. That was always a pleasant thing, at any rate, the walk in the High Street. He did not meet the usual people, they were away mostly; but still there were a fair number of pretty girls to keep up the reputation of the street—for nowhere in London can you see so many pretty women as in Kensington High Street near the church at a quarter to one o'clock in the afternoon. He had come home to fetch something, instead of lunching close by the office. He was wishing that he could always just take a light-hearted appreciative pleasure in looking at the pretty girls as they passed, and not have a pain, a kind of twinge, and an absurd wish to go out of his way to see them again (which, by the way, he seldom did). Sometimes he felt so; quite pleased without a drawback, glad without a thought of melancholy; but it was only rarely.

Suddenly he met his friend Miss Spencer. She was astonished to find him still in town. She was infinitely kind, and could not see this boy alone in London without wanting to do something for him. So she asked him to come in on Thursday afternoon. "Miss Lemardelay has promised to come," she added.

It was very kind of Miss Spencer to take pity on him; but he did not know that he was very eager to go and see her. It was true she was a dear old lady, and he thought he might get on well enough with her alone; but he had never felt at ease in her house, which was the meeting-place of a number of distinguished artistic people, a set whose members seemed to George to be sloesly bound together against outsiders—"creepy" people he and his brothers always called them. And Helen Lemardelay, who was to be at Miss Spencer's, was the only child of the most renowned and wonderful lady in this set. He had been introduced again and again to Mrs. Lemardelay and she never recognised him. Helen he had met constantly at Miss Spencer's house in the Campden Hill Road, she almost lived there when Margaret, Miss Spencer's niece, was staying with her aunt. George admired both the girls, but felt afraid of them, especially of Helen, who reflected some of the wonder of her mother; and Mrs. Lemardelay frightened George very much with the poetical halo which she carried with her. He used to try and imagine sometimes what kind of life this wonderful woman and daughter led in their beautiful house hidden behind the high wall of Wright's Lane. George would never have the courage to ask Helen Lemardelay to dance with him when he saw her at a ball; she was so superior and always appeared so much at home in the houses where he met her— running off with Margaret upstairs into unknown bedrooms to fetch something, or going into supper with a distinguished painter. He imagined that the conversations in which she took part must be peculiarly interesting and out of the common. And then she was one among a number of girl-friends who liked being together, and who had their own jokes and occupation, while he was on the outside.

George went on Thursday. Helen Lemardelay was already in the drawing-room when he arrived. He felt a little afraid as Miss Spencer walked across the room with him to where she was sitting. She was so wonderful—and the last time he had seen her was at a dance where he had not dared to ask her to dance with him.

The three talked for some time, and then Miss Spencer mentioned the shade in the garden, and asked them whether they would not go out—

"I'm afraid I don't know where the tennis things are."

They both protested that they did not want to play; but they stood up and Miss Lemardelay led the way through the window,

8

brushing past the hanging creeper, and down the few steps. At the bottom she waited and looked back. George followed her, astonished to find himself alone with Helen Lemardelay, as he might have been with any ordinary girl. She must think him a dull outsider; but still here she was, he would have to say something not too uninteresting, and it would be exciting to see what she was like separated from her usual surroundings. He began the conversation safely by asking if she had heard from Margaret Spencer lately.

"Yes, I got a letter yesterday. She says your friends the Bishops are in Dieppe, and apparently they see a good deal of one another."

"Do you know Henry Bishop at all well?" "No; I hardly think I've ever spoken to him.

He was at Trinity with you, wasn't he?"

"Yes."

Then there was a short pause as they walked side by side along the gravel path. Then they talked for some time of other friends, and of dances, of theatres, of the season which had just finished.

"I'm surprised to find you still in London," George said, in order to become personal.

"My mother wasn't well enough to go away; she's getting better. But it's rather dreary in London now, isn't it?"

"Yes, it is. I'm staying in town because I've some work to do on an evening paper—a chance not to be missed."

"Oh, you're a journalist? Well, it can't be so dull for you if you've your work."

"My work doesn't interest me much—not enough at any rate to fill up the whole day."

9

"What do you have to do?" she said, as they turned the corner of the lawn.

"I have to muddle about and arrange things chiefly; now and then I do a bit of my own."

"You don't write criticisms?"

"One or two. But there aren't many to be done now. Besides, chattering about other people's novels and pictures is nothing to look forward to."

"You don't write novels or stories yourself?" "No. I thought I might when I was a boy—we all do, I believe. But I can't. And besides, novels—even if one could write them—that wouldn't be enough. Fancy going about all day and all your life wondering how to work out a story: there's something so false about it: and Art, Art, I'm sick of it."

The young man ended rather hotly, and was afraid directly that he had been unnecessarily vehement—especially as he was talking to a girl who was almost a stranger—so he went on. "However" ... and stopped.

"It's ten minutes to five, Helen, and you said you wished to get home to your mother by five," Miss Spencer called from the balcony.

Helen turned and held out her hand to George.

"Well, I must be going, Mr. Aston. Will you come and see us, as you're all alone? You know where we live? Today is Thursday: come next Saturday, will you? Good-bye."

She walked away, leaving George at the bottom of the steps, ashamed of himself. And as he walked home he was vexed that he had spoken all the time about himself, in the regular young man's fashion to a girl whom he hardly knew. She had only been making conversation, and did not want serious discussions. And then later on in the evening, when he was sitting alone, he wondered whether after all what he had said was true. Had he not exaggerated? He could not recall the conversation exactly; but his impression was that he had bored the girl for a long time with the causes of his melancholy, which was not the case. "She must think me a great lumbering fool," he said aloud as he got into bed—which was not the case either, for she did not think much about him.

III.

MRS. LEMARDELAY was a great person, very well known in Kensington: well known, in fact, everywhere where artists predominated, or persons who called themselves artistic. She was, at the time of which we are speaking, a little over fifty, and her masses of dull red hair were patched with grey.

Thirty years before, Clara Simpson, the daughter of a small tradesman, had been the ideal of a small renowned set of painters and poets. Her hair, her pale complexion, and a certain languour in her movements, made these poets and painters rave. When she was thirty, to the astonishment of her friends, she married Henry Lemardelay, an Englishman in business in the City, connected with the great French banking family of Lemardelay. He was a quiet, stiff man who for once in his life had fallen madly in love, and with Clara Simpson. Her friends, of course, expected that she would marry one of her interesting admirers. But comradeship does not lead necessarily to marriage, and few of her admirers had two thousand a year then.

In a manner Clara Simpson had deceived the world; the deception was quite unconscious. The school of painters and poets who had made her famous by their admiration of her personal appearance would hardly have asked themselves whether she was really the wonderful person of their representations. They had the intelligence, she gave the material: the result pleased them and gradually the public. Therefor Clara Simpson appeared first to the world as the mysterious and wonderful woman who inspired a whole set of artists. And she looked the character perfectly. Moreover, she had a safeguard against detection in her extreme indolence. The indolence of a tall, beautiful woman, with a strange and poetical face, shows remarkably like superior intelligence. She spoke little, very rarely made a mistake, the magnificence of her appearance, and again her extraordinary idleness, combined to give the effect of some hidden purpose. She had no sense of humour. A common characteristic of beautiful stupid people who have been very much petted when they were young, is a certain kind of callousness. For instance, Mrs. Lemardelay lived in comfort in a beautiful old house with a big garden, and she enjoyed it. But if she had suddenly become poor, she would have borne the misfortune well, better than most people. If only she were left in peace, allowed to go to bed early, and get up late, and live undisturbed, she would be contented. She had a narrow circle of vision: but as she did not try to understand anything outside the circle (the greater part of which was taken up by her own easy-going self) her limitations were not apparent.

During the afternoon of Friday Mrs. Lemardelay had a visit from an old admirer. He was a painter of about her age, and had been the chief friend and pupil of the great man of the movement. He often came to the Lemardelay's, and sat talking and laughing with the lady of the house, chiefly about old times. Helen objected to him. As to his pictures, she had no sense for painting; and of all pictures she disliked most those of his school. Her mother had been the inspiration of a large part of the movement, and that in her mind made it worse: she knew nothing of other artists; but the set to which her mother belonged annoyed, even at times disgusted her. There was something so selfish, it seemed to her, in the way in which they talked and lived—unworldly yet selfish. For their pictures and poems had nothing to do with the world, and she was annoyed that her mother should not be a centre of a movement which was not only selfish, but which was really a thing of the past. She was annoyed with these self-satisfied people who chattered and mutually supported themselves with admiration, while the world, the people who really worked, had gone right past and were doing something else—even if they ever had really admired this

way of thinking, which she could hardly believe. Her exceedingly upright and rather puritanical nature revolted. If she had
been with the more serious and sympathetic members of the set,
she might have been less vehement in her dislike. But her objection was unmitigated, because in the life of her mother, the idle
person whom they all admired, she could see no justification of
their ways. These feelings seemed to be the whole cause of her
dissatisfaction, she could not see any further: and her objection
had lately gone so far that she was irritated even at the pretty
sleepy house in which they lived, irritated at the pictures and the
artistic furniture, at the dark rooms overshadowed by vine and
clematis.

This afternoon she found Mr. Withers more unbearable than
ever. She sat at the tea-table while he and her mother laughed
at a common acquaintance.

"And my daughter Iseult has gone the same way. Of course I
didn't mind so long as she and her brother kept to pottery They
made some very pretty bowls and things. But now she has followed the rest of our young people and become a violent socialist. The two things seem to go together. If they didn't bother
me so, I should be amused. Our children have degenerated. We
are artists; we started a great school and painted pictures, but
our children can only get as far as pots and carpets. Naturally
they have to eke out their pots with socialism. It's the tail end.
I only wish they would be quiet, and amuse themselves without
troubling other people. But when once a man, and especially a
women, becomes altruistic, moral, social—he or she can't leave
other people alone... I hope," he added, turning to Helen with
smile which she thought patronising, "I hope our Miss Helen
won't behave in this ridiculous manner?"

His speech and the tone of his voice had thoroughly annoyed
her, and his last words made her indignant. She answered
hotly—

"I don't see any reason for sneering at people because they are not selfish."

The man had looked at her as he finished his question, but seeing her resentment he immediately looked away: and now, without taking notice of what Helen had said, he spoke to Mrs. Lemardelay in an uninterested tone of voice——"

"The Fishers have gone to live at Chelsea."

It made Helen's position unbearable; she was absolutely ignored, treated like a child, and had to sit still after she had been slighted, and listen to this man prating to her mother. And yet to get up and go away would be absurd. It was all the more exasperating because what he said was so heartless and unconcerned, so inhuman: and yet it seemed to her typical of all this way of life which disgusted her. She did not much care for Iseult, did not know her at all well, and thought it rather silly of her to make pots over which all the people raved. But this new development, this socialism pleased her. After- all it did show some amount of unselfishness, some humanity and interest in life. It was a relief from the narrow life of her mother's best friends, and for a father to sneer and be cool about it seemed unpardonable. But how could an artist be unselfish and work for other people, she argued. The nature of his employment made him entirely personal, and closed his eyes to everything but his own narrow sphere of isolated work. Mr. Withers behaved as if the only reality in life lay in the work and narrow interests of his set; everything else in the world was only part of an absurd comedy, to be laughed at and spoken of lightly. And all her inartistic, moral nature rose in fresh revolt, so that she though that she would hardly be able to hide her feelings.

She had been thinking angrily for herself, and had not noticed the conversation which was going on. She was brought back again by seeing the gentleman rise to say good-bye. After he had shaken hands with Mrs. Lemardelay, who was lying in convalescent style on a long wicker chair, he turned to Helen and held out his hand. Helen always had irritated him; but he had almost forgotten that anything particular had happened this time, so he said nothing to her. If he had shown that he was still thinking of what he had said, she would probably have given expression to the thought to which her reverie had led—"Anyhow, it's our turn which is coming now!" But he said nothing, so she too was silent. When he was gone, she felt more comfortable. She knew that her mother would not begin any conversation upon what had happened. That was characteristic of Mrs. Lemardelay; she seldom bothered any one. Moreover, she rather mistrusted herself with her daughter, and would not enter into a realm where she might find difficulties. And so the two sat on in silence, until Helen's thoughts led her to day suddenly—

"Mother, I've asked Mr. Aston to come in to tea to-morrow. I met him on Thursday at Miss Spencer's. He's rather dull all alone here: staying for his work.'

"Is he that rather sentimental looking young man who danced a good deal with Miss Bishop at the Spencers' a month ago?"

"Yes; he's a friend of the Bishop's."

IV.

SATURDAY came, and George was thinking a good deal of his visit. The day passed away quickly. As he turned down Wright's Lane he felt uncomfortably shy. He had always been so afraid of these people! And as he pulled the long iron bell-handle and looked at the two white balls at the top of the gate pillars, and the gas lamp in the middle, he grew still more afraid. The gate went with a click. He pushed it open and walked along the path and up the steps of the house.

Mrs. Lemardelay would be sure not to recognise him: she was not well. He had come only on her daughter's invitation. The hall was rather dark, furnished with old furniture. Everything was very quiet. He felt still more afraid.

As he entered the drawing-room Helen came forward and shook hands with him. Mrs. Lemardelay said, "How do you do, Mr. Aston? Isn't it hot? We will have some tea at once." then, after a few words about the weather, she went on—"You didn't know Miss Spencer's step-brother Vincent, I suppose? He was a very promising young painter. Do you like the pictures of his which she has in her house?"

"They are certainly very interesting!" And Mrs. Lemardelay and George went on, George agreeing with all she said. Helen now and then put in a word.

He left the house, the visit was over. There was something unsatisfactory about it. He had expected a great deal, for some reason. He had hardly spoken to Helen; but what a face she had! He had never looked at her so closely before, although he had known her ever since he was seventeen. The fair brown hair, a shade darker than her pale brown colouring, gave her face a look of complete harmony; and he had not noticed before how blue and fearless her eyes were. He had a pleasant and engrossing subject for his thoughts now.

The very next day, Sunday, the first day of August, he was in Portland Road Station, waiting for a train to take him west. As he was walking up the platform he noticed her coming down the steps and through the gate in front of him. She turned round and saw him, and they shook hands. She had hardly told him that she was going to High Street, when an Addison Road train came in noisily, and stopped further conversation. They stood back and watched the passengers get out and in. The train moved on and left the platform still and almost empty. They walked a few steps side by side in silence. Suddenly she turned to him a laughing face, and said—

"You don't really admire Vincent Spencer's pictures, do you?"

"No, I don't."

"You only said you did out of politeness to my mother? I don't know why I thought so, for you didn't show it—but I was sure it was so."

This gave George an intimate pleasure, and made them both feel very friendly. She had remembered what he had said, recognised his position, and sided with him against her mother.

She laughed again, and said—

"You talked a great deal about art, for a person who professes to hate it! When you told me on Thursday that you hated it, it didn't make much effect on me. But I remembered it on Saturday."

"Well, what was I to do?

18

She was so friendly and pleasant that he felt quite willing to put himself entirely into her hands.

"Oh, I'm not blaming you. Only you won't go on being polite to me, will you? Besides, I hate art as much as you do; more, I expect, because I daresay you understand about it. I start unsympathetic, and then I'm annoyed with it."

"But how extraordinary that you of all people should be like this!"

"Do you think so?"

It was such an exquisite pleasure for both of them to be beginning each other in this way. They felt like children early in the morning digging in some new soil.

The train came in and stopped them. They did not have such interesting talk afterwards. As they parted she said—

"Come and see us soon—some tomorrow, won't you, as you've no one to go home to? And you needn't be afraid of my mother. She doesn't really care about pictures or opinions or that kind of thing."

He went to see them the next day. And after that he came every day to tea, turning the corner of Wright's Lane on leaving the station as if that had been his habit for years. It seemed to him quite natural that he should be at Wright's Lane every afternoon. There was something gorgeous to his mind in their solitude; he knew that in time his mother and his people and his friends would come back, Helen and her mother would go away for a week or two when she was strong enough, and then all her friends would surround her once more. Meanwhile they were absolutely alone. They both took an extravagant delight in the feeling that they were more interested in each other than in anything else, and that their friends knew nothing of the matter, and were of no importance in their minds— the world with its ordinary life stood still while they enjoyed the magical familiarity which had suddenly grown between them.

A short time before the threatened departure of the Lemardelays, Helen and George were walking in the garden as usual. Day after day during the hot August they had found no difficulty in continuing their conversation; if there were differences of opinion they were no subject for opposition or argument, they seemed rather to be converging to meet at some point. They had been talking seriously and eagerly, and George found that he was telling her of himself very closely, and went on in a lighter tone, conversational, so as to hide his real seriousness.

"Have you ever felt that kind of causeless melancholy? For it must be causeless—I never hear of any one absolutely sickened of life because he couldn't express an idea! Especially as I do not want to express the thing. Have you a recipe for the cure of it? I could understand bearing up and being cheerful under misfortune—but when there's no misfortune! The usual advice, 'Cheer up, the luck will turn,' is good enough and could be followed under a calamity, but in this case what's to be done? Have you a recipe?"

She was an attentive and apt learner. No, she had not felt quite that—dissatisfaction certainly, but not quite that. A feeling of revolt, but against something actual which she disliked. She explained a little her objection to the surroundings in which she lived, as she had begun to do at Portland Road.

"But have you no friends, didn't you find men at college who could help you? I find that a woman like Margaret Spencer is always by me when I'm low-spirited or disgusted, and she helps me in her gentle way—but I understand you: yes, I understand you," she added, eager and pleased.

"Well, with my friends, you see, it's like this. There's always a kind of pose about such friendships. We don't perhaps care for each other; but we discuss theories, art, philosophy. But I

wanted something much more simple and direct, something af-
fectionate, intimate. No pose, no obstacles, so theories—purely
human intimacy. I don't want 'to think the same about the state'
or about anything else, or to differ: I don't want to think at all,
but simply to chatter and be comfortable and filled up, humanly
and affectionately. I want something to guard me against myself
and against the empty melancholy. I see sometimes that it's ridiculous—I can even laugh at it; but what's the use of that? It
remains all the same." Here was a direct appeal, a cry which
moved her. He added quickly—

"I don't want to exaggerate: sometimes it's gay. But I want
something permanent. I should be ashamed if I thought I was
magnifying my trouble to you. ... But no, no, I don't think I
am—and, as far as I can see, no work will serve the purpose."

And to this appeal she found an answer, a sublime answer.
She hardly knew what she was saying: she had never thought it
out before, never clearly, at least. But here was some one who
demanded something of her, needed her help; and her wisdom
came to meet the need: suddenly it was there, suddenly she knew.

"The only recipe for melancholy which can't be fought
against is a patience upheld by the knowledge that others are
suffering the same. In your dreary times, in your agony—ridiculous though you say it is, yet I understand—in your trouble, just
think of others of your age, boys or girls, who are suffering in the
same way. And you will have a large warm rising in your heart, a
feeling of brotherhood, a feeling that we are all the same—and
that would give patience... wouldn't it?" She finished, becoming a little timid and astonished at herself towards the end,
turning her face to his tentatively after her great exposition,
with an exquisite look in her eyes.

He almost gasped, he called out her name, he could not say
anything more: he could only have fallen at her feet. For a few
seconds he gazed at her while she looked away over the trees. It

did not seem as if they were in the ordinary world and could act in the ordinary way. How they had sprung to meet at the first touch! She made a step and he cried out, clasping his hands—

"Oh, stop! Stay still! Let me look at you." She made another step, and said—

"No, not now, I'll go in. Come again soon—to- morrow," and she walked to the house, just casting one glance at him and meeting his eye. Her look was serious, thoughtful—almost respectful. He did not follow her.

She went away. She felt a little uncertain— what it was she did not know. Perhaps an undefined feeling that they had suddenly come so close that nothing further was possible except that he should kneel at her feet and worship, and she should raise him up and tell him that she was not to be worshipped—he himself had put this into her: it was his own... as she was.

And she sat in her room and wondered and wondered. Suddenly how great! How new! Nothing could disgust her now. If Iseult's father had come and talked again, she would not have become indignant. Not because she would agree anymore; but it would not concern her personally: she was above it. She had now her own personal work. Here was something to do, something to be unselfish about, something clear and beautiful, far above the troubles which she had endured. Then she thought of George, of his looks, of his character which she knew. But how sudden! And she laughed gently to herself. She could give him exactly what he wanted.

And he too went home in ecstasy. The whole difficulty had been swept away. In an hour it was gone so completely that he could hardly comprehend what it was that had troubled him. She, this exquisitely fair figure, had come with sympathy. In herself she was enough. And with her she brought this wonderful new gospel that had sounded so gorgeous in his ears—and this gospel she had invented for him. And he remembered her timid, inquiring look as she said, "That would give, patience, wouldn't it?" And then he fell to thinking of her sweetness and her beauty. And then, in remembering every detail, he came back to her teaching. How grand it sounded. And it had been given just when it was wanted; and how it had been given! It was no piece of morality. She had not learnt it. No, she had discovered a wonderful gospel, and discovered it solely for him. Some such doctrine as this he had certainly heard before; but it had never meant anything to him, a statement which did not apply, unaccompanied by proof or means of fulfilment. There was even an entry in his Cambridge diary the day after his return from a dance in London: he was sitting dreaming, his mind filled with vague longings, the pleasant-looking porter brought him up a letter, and he imagined the man looking into his eyes with a friendly glance, and saying, "At it again, young man? Yes, I know, we all go through it"—but it had remained a pretty thing on paper.

When Helen came down for dinner, she noticed a letter on the hall-table from France which she had not seen before. It was from Margaret, telling her of Dieppe. After a few words about her newly-married sister, Mrs. Forde, with whom she was staying, she went on—

"I have taken a fancy to Henry Bishop—that is to say, as far as I can see him through the absurd theoretical extravagances which I suppose will pass away, and only belong to his youthfulness. He is just finishing a story, and he talks a great deal about art. You know that I never quite understand all these enthusiasms for abstract things. I am very glad that books are written and pictures painted—and I suppose writers and painters must have somebody to bother with their theories and despondencies: only a bother it certainly is. The books and pictures are very well when they are done, and they form a pleasant part of life then; but when the manufacture of them engrosses so much of life, that seems to me to a mistake. I daresay older men manage the affair better. They write their books in work hours, quietly, and we enjoy them; but in between they are human and not abstract. I hope you do not find your artistic surroundings too unbearable. However much I laugh at—or rather, however little I understand— enthusiasm for opinions, and ravings about Ibsen and Wagner or socialism—remember (of course you will) that I have never laughed at you or wanted to laugh when I saw your dislike to your life at home. You put it sometimes as an abstract affair; but somehow it was not irrelevant, or not so irrelevant as the abstract extravagances as these young men. You were personal and human, these people miss the point—and it looks unreal with them. This essay, which I am just finishing for your edification, all comes from having been so much with Mr. Bishop————"

Helen sat down before her writing-case to answer her Margaret's letter. They had been close friends since high-school days. Often Helen, in her girlish moods of revolt, when she was harassed by principles, had found peace in the calm content of Margaret. Her gentle laughter, and half-assumed incapacity for understanding any searchings of heart whatever, made Helen also easier. They had never had a secret from one another, and they had often talked of the kind of men whom they would love, and of how they would manage things. Helen began her letter apologetically. She felt a sudden yearning for Margaret, an inexpressible tenderness towards her. So she began by saying that she was afraid she was still liable to enthusiasms and discontent and abstract leadings. And, moreover, she hinted that Margaret was not with her to bring her back to content—and suppose some one appeared who justified her revolt? She had wanted something which her life at home could not give her, what it was she could not tell; but the want was comprehensible enough. "I want to be doing something; and my surroundings seem to me to be selfish. My wish would lead me to some kind of sacrifice; but a strong sacrifice, a sacrifice which is needed, and which would use all my good qualities— perhaps sacrifice is not the right word, for I suppose it would be a sacrifice to give in to my mother's life entirely; but above all things I wish to get away, to get free of the whole atmosphere, and never hear of art again. I want to do." She would not say anything about George Aston— she did not know how to tell the truth. Besides, it would not be fair to him—and then she thought, "Perhaps I do not know myself exactly what it means;" she would have to wait till she saw him again. A long reverie interrupted her writing.

When she had finished the letter to Margaret she wrote to Iseult, for she felt now quite sympathetic towards her. She had for a long time been ready to become interested in social and moral questions, for they seemed the natural escape from art. But she was only willing, nothing more; she needed a leading force somewhere, a reason to move her to actual doing. In course of time, perhaps, especially if she had been asked to bear many conversations with Iseult's father, she might have made a start. But now she felt a need in George Aston's need, her revolt had a justification. She would boldly help all the world; but she began now because here she saw the way to help one who had appealed to her personally. It seemed to her as if that day for the first time had an opportunity been given her of entering on the life for which she was fitted. What she felt was not merely a fancy for this man, was not an ordinary attachment; in fact, she did not know whether those words would apply to her at all. No, it was an explanation of her whole life up to now, it was the meaning of the world, the justification of all her wishes, and such a justification as made the wishes clear, brought them out of hidden corners and put them forward, pulled together so many loose and scattered thoughts and feelings into one whole as almost to create a new character. They had known each other by sight for a long time, and had met often, and even talked now and then; but hardly had they caught a glimpse of what they really were, when they sprang to meet each other.

George went down to the office next morning his thoughts full of her. He was filled with wonder as he thought over the events of that afternoon, and at moments he did not know how to understand his relations to Helen; but then he thought of her face and the meaning look which he had last seen upon it—a kind of seriousness which promised a continuance of the intimacy which had so suddenly sprung up between them—and when he remembered her face he felt reassured. As usual he went to lunch with five or six other men on the staff. He had done so the very day before; but he was astonished that they were still telling tales of how some one had been drunk and could not write a proper article, or some one else had done something else; they still were chaffing one another as before, and he wondered how it could still amuse them, as if he had been away for years. A discussion which arose between them reminded him that a few months ago, when he was at Cambridge, art and morality, the last act of the Doll's House, programme music, and such things, had been a real trouble. Fancy, he remembered one occasion when he was quite restless because he had been shown a picture which evidently depended for its full appreciation upon literary sentiment. This had destroyed his peace of mind! And only a few weeks before the expression of an idea had brought him to despair. It was incomprehensible. How could he have tormented himself over such things?

At half-past five he was again at Wright's Lane. Helen met him with the same look of respect, almost deference, in her eyes. He had doubted at moments whether they would be able to meet at the point at which they had parted; but directly he saw her he recognised that in his doubt he had reckoned without her. They could not be quite as intimate as on that afternoon, but he was assured that she had taken their actions in its full seriousness.

"Helen and I are going to the seaside for three weeks at the end of next week, Mr. Aston. Will you have to stay in London?" Mrs. Lemardelay asked.

"Yes. My man does not come back for quite another fortnight. And even then I hope I shall be able to find work enough on the paper to keep me here."

"You know the Withers, don't you?" Helen asked.

"No, not really. I've met Philip once or twice."

She smiled at him, and put her hand out upon the table at her side.

"Philip, you know, and Iseult have meetings on Saturday evenings. They get a fair number of people to come, and some of them speak very well. She often asked me to come to a meeting, but I've never cared enough to go till now" (it was a delight to her to be quite bold and to speak the absolute truth to him, especially when her mother was by); "but now I should like to go if you'll go with me, next Saturday? I wrote to Iseult and said that I'd come perhaps, trusting that you'd take me."

"I'd certainly love to go. Yes, do let us go by all means," he said warmly, and he would have liked to get up and take hold of the hand which had been stretched out to the table when the request was begun. When his eyes met hers he smiled happily at her; there was a look of such directness and strength and freedom in her face as it was turned to his. Mrs.

Lemardelay was a little astonished at this change in her daughter. She had generally been dull and uninterested with men; but now she was easy. She was leading, cheerfully, and confidently. It came natural to Helen to be so with him; in fact, there was no question with her as to her behaviour towards him. It simply was so.

When she had made this arrangement with him she was satisfied. That was enough, and she sat contentedly in her chair.

"Then you'll come and fetch me a little before eight?" she said, as he went. She did not wish to have him to dinner first. It would be so much nicer if he came and fetched her straight away.

V.

AT the end of July, when George Aston had been left alone in the house, the dreariness of his surroundings had seemed to him natural and fitting. The empty house, with its lifeless rooms, was the only and complete accompaniment to his own dreariness. In the evenings he sat alone in the dining-room. Between eleven and twelve he shut the window and the shutters, locked the front door, put out the gas, lit his candle, and marched up the uncarpeted stairs. When his people were at home, there had always been a reunion in the dining-room before bedtime. There had been cake or biscuit eating, water drinking, a joke or two, and "good- nights." Now it was all solemn and solitary— naturally.

Since the appearance of Helen that Thursday afternoon at Miss Spencer's, the idea of her was a balm to his spirits. Everything suddenly became bright. She filled his thoughts, and for the first time he had something clear and legitimate to think of, and at all times. His unfounded dreams and romances, which had begun as far back as he could remember, far back in his childhood, were over.

For a long time they had ceased to excite him; but still he had changed and changed them about cunningly, in order to keep up his interest.

But now the dreams were done with for ever: here was a strong, actual personality facing him— here, right in front of him; and the romances which he had twisted to suit his fancy had gone. And with them the trouble of his desires was finished too. This human being, with beauty and life and character of her own, had stilled them.

He had wondered sometimes if the muddy troubled water could ever become clear; and if not, how he would come shrink away if any one, if any woman, saw into it. No effort of his own could purge it. But now that he knew her, it was calm and limpid. The saving grace had come in time.

But he did not feel inferior. She knew he was not a worthless person. Only there was something weighing him down; and he needed help to get himself free. He had found it in a fair companionship. If she looked into him now, she would find him clear; and if she were to know what he had been before, she would know that she herself had cleared him of something which was not part of himself, she herself had done it, and that would be enough. So he thought to himself.

Saturday came. It was a fine, warm evening. "I think we might go by omnibus, don't you?

Take the blue omnibus to Fulham road, and then the white?

They walked in silence to the corner of the road, and waited for their omnibus. Up they climbed to the top, George feeling how delightful it was to have a companion. When they were settled in their seats he began at once to talk of that afternoon in the garden. They had not been alone since then. His boldness was dashed with a little timidity.

"Since that afternoon in your garden the whole thing has changed," he said, putting the matter broadly in his shyness. Helen was glad, too, that they were able to go back to that subject; she knew how much had he had meant to express by the rather awkward and inexpressive sentence, and she answered simply—

"It has made a great difference to me."

These two needed only the exchange of a few words in order to become at once deliciously familiar. They talked on about that afternoon, and then they were silent for some little time.

They had very nearly reached the bottom of Redcliffe Gardens. During this silence they both began to feel so pleased and light-hearted, that they knew the next thing to come would be something over which they could both laugh thoroughly. George began laughing first, and she, already smiling, turned to him for a reason.

"I used to be afraid of you." "Really. Why?"

The omnibus swung round to the other side of the road and stopped.

George and Helen got off and walked to the opposite side of Fulham Road.

"Where do the Withers live exactly?" he asked.

"In the middle of the Hurlingham Road. Do you know where that is?"

"No."

"Well, we go along the road till we nearly reach Putney Bridge, then we turn left. They live in a house called the Vineyard—a pretty old house."

"But Mr. Withers lives in Melbury Road——" "Yes, he and his wife and younger son live there. But Iseult and her brother came down here and took the old house, which had been to let for a long time. It's very pretty, and it suited them well, because it's close to their pottery works in Wandsworth."

It was still quite light, the sky was green up the road, and the lamps were just being lit," The omnibus came along the street. When they were seated on the top, she began laughing again where she had left off, and said—

"But why were you afraid of me?"

"I'd always heard a great deal about you, about you and your mother. I saw you first quite a long time ago, but I only met you at rather long intervals, and then always at houses where you were very much at home, surrounded by friends, talking to distinguished people, and I was an outsider. Everybody knew you, and talked to you; I wasn't one of them; I never felt quite easy at those houses, and I hardly thought you would recognise me, as we so seldom talked to each other."

"I seemed to you to be quite one of the clique——"

"Yes, he interrupted; "and a clique peculiarly artistic and poetical; rather out of the world in their pose; decidedly pleased with a closer bond than any other set of people that I know of—I knew the Cambridge branch a little."

She gave a peal of laughter—

"Why, you talk as if it were a bank!"

"Well, as I say, I often felt awkward among you;"—(he said "you" on purpose, because they were both in such high spirits)—"but I took it out in being amused sometimes, when I was away and thinking of the whole thing. I've even stood still all alone in the midst of Trinity Street, and shouted aloud with laughter."

They both joined in a long laugh. She answered—

"You see now that I'm not so closely bound up with them. I naturally sailed along with the stream, and if I objected to our clique often enough, that wouldn't appear when we were out in society. At a party, it's exceedingly pleasant to know every one, and to feel at home, even if every one isn't very charming."

"I've no doubt we were often absolutely rude to strangers. I shouldn't think of defending myself to you; you're quite right, and you know what I am now."

Then she went on—it was her turn—

"I daresay I appeared extra cliquey to you because I never cared particularly for the company of young men. I've no brothers, nor has Margaret; and I never knew any boys at all well. Whereas I had a number of girlfriends, and we were very fond of each other, and had a hundred different points of contact. It was an easy, intimate friendship with them, and it hardly seemed worth while to take the trouble of getting over the initial difficulty with boys. Some girls whom I knew always got on very well with boys and young men; but I never quite understood how they did it—and they happened to be girls I didn't much like. I was rather narrow-minded; but I find it very difficult to remember that there are difference ways of living life."

They talked on with great pleasure and ease until Helen told George that they must get down at the next turning.

"This way," Helen said. George had never been in that part before; but Helen knew all about it, she was taking him.

Once off the omnibus and walking in the street, they began talking about more obvious things.

"I daresay this meeting won't amuse you particularly; but it will be rather interesting to see what they are about. I object to Mr. Withers, the father, so I naturally have a leaning towards the son and daughter whom he disapproves of."

"The father Withers is one of the strongest members of the set, isn't he?"

"Yes, he is. Well, I never liked him! The other day he came to call and he talked in such a superior way about his art, and Iseult's folly in becoming a socialist."

They walked down a short street of little unquiet red-brick houses, laughing at the names— Englemere, Dunkeld, Mowddyr, until they reached a narrow road at right angles. A long wall ran down one side, and on the other were some more little red- brick houses. In the centre of them stood the Vineyard, somewhat back from the road. In the daytime it looked very pretty, white and green woodwork round the windows, and a disused stable with a handsome cobble pavement at the side. They went through the gate and knocked. Philip himself opened the door.

"How splendid of you to come," he said to Helen; "and how do you do?" shaking hands with Aston. "I think the last time we met was at the Spencers'?"

He was dressed in a dark brown velvet coat and black trousers, and wore a dark red tie and roll- down collar. The hall of the house was empty, handsome with broad tiled floor, a magnificent carpet on the walls, and a long white deal settee standing against one side.

They went into the dining-room. This was empty also. There was no carpet on the white deal floor. Over the fireplace there was some fine ornamentation which Philip had discovered under paint and had restored with great care himself. The wainscotting was high, and the walls were covered with a cream-coloured paper stamped in gold; a piece of it was old, the rest he had practically made himself, for he had supervised the manufacture at some works not far off. The table, upon which were the remains of a supper, was lighted by a lamp with silver reflectors. There were some dozen people in the room, men and women, talking and laughing loudly. As Philip entered with the two visitors, Iseult came forward and greeted Helen, and was introduced to George. They stood aside, Helen and Iseult talking, and George standing by. Philip joined the others, and continued the joke which had been interrupted by the knock at the door. It was some technical point about a lecture which one of their number, a Fabian, had delivered a day or two before. George had never heard of the man, and did not understand what they were all laughing at; but they evidently delighted to be talking about their own business.

After a few minutes Philip said—

"Well, come on, you people, we must be moving."

Iseult explained to Helen that they now had their meetings at the pottery works. The numbers had increased, and they found that some of the work-men and their friends came to the works more willingly than to their house, and felt more comfortable. As the people began to move out of the room, George recognised a man whom he had known slightly at Cambridge. He had been at King's, and was already in his third year when George was a freshman. George had known of him chiefly as one of the Cambridge secretaries of Toynbee Hall and a strong teetotaler. When he saw George, he shook hands with him, as an old hand welcomes a beginner.

"Ah, Aston, are you coming to join us? If I remember, at Cambridge you had the reputation of being a scoffer at 'things social and moral,' and you were a great authority on art. Have you found out the emptiness of your desires?" he added, laughingly, as he turned to answer the question of a Russian who was at his side.

George was irritated at this. The remark was true; but he did not want to be patronised by this man whom he had despised at Cambridge. He was still sore from his particular troubles, and this self- satisfied young person, who was familiar with the country George was about to explore, could not understand how he felt.

Helen was standing by, and had heard what the man said. This whole visit was so entirely her own venture and for George's sake, that she was peculiarly sensitive for him; she understood

34

exactly what he was feeling, and even forestalled him. He belonged to her for the time being. She slipped her hand softly into his arm. This first movement of familiarity, showing the most delicate sympathy, would have atoned for much more. He looked at her, their eyes met; he laughed, partly at himself, partly from delight—a gentle laugh in which she joined, and they walked out together with the others.

"The dining-room and the hall are the only parts of the house which we have finished yet. We are doing things gradually. We shall have terrible work with the garden—the house has been to let for so long."

"How far off are the works?"

"Just down the road to the left, not more than five minutes' walk."

They left the house and trooped along the road. Iseult greatly pleased and not a little astonished at Helen's visit, not quite knowing what this sudden kindness meant, walked behind with George and Helen. She felt that something generous and good was going on, she did not know what; but it made her feel kindly towards Helen and her friend. She spoke very sweetly to Helen and quite won her heart.

Iseult's nature was really sensitive to an extraordinary degree. She was retiring, and sometimes appeared timid; the last person to be in any way an innovator, or to take a strong line, a careless observer would have thought. But it was the conscientious side of this very sensitiveness which had forced her into a position apparently unsuited to her gentle nature. She had suffered much from her father's opposition; but all the more, her sensitive conscience led her to be firm—more impenetrably firm even than the strong people. The thing she could bear least was the struggle with persons—always less sensitive than herself—whom she loved. And when she could oppose them no longer, she would desist and remain silent, and appear afterwards, having done her way: so that some people thought she was not straightforward. It was the impossibility felt by a sensitive nature either of bearing opposition beyond a certain point of giving in. When they reached the big workshop, they found half a dozen men and two women already there. Philip Withers spoke first. He began about the long hours. Then he showed how long hours were worse now when everything was done by machinery than they used to be in the old days of apprenticeship, when a man became interested in his work. Then he went on to the evils of machinery. Nowadays a worker only knew how to make one little motion with his hand. If that occupation failed him, he was useless. Further, these enormous factories had tended to put middlemen between the consumer and the maker, whereas the small intelligent craftsmen used to sell his work himself. And besides, there was the important fact that the factory-made things were bad and ugly.

When he had finished, a little old man, a hump-back, with long grey beard and keen face, got up to bear witness to the truth of what Withers had said. He was a bootmaker, and his experience was that he gained more by retailing a ready-made boot than by making a thirty-shilling pair of boots himself. Was it surprising that people because middlemen rather than workers? The boot trade was so bad, that no apprentices cared to come and learn the work; soon people would have quite forgotten how to make a good pair of boots by hand. And as Mr. Withers had said, when they were finished, the ready-made boots were bad and ugly. Other men spoke. Between the speeches the King's man and one or two others continued a discussion about an abtruse point in the history of communism, talking rather loudly and with a good many epigrams, as if they were superior to the ordinary business of the meeting—they had heard that kind of thing so often.

After the meeting was over George and Helen stayed behind with Iseult to look at some designs which they were trying to carry out at the works. Then they went back to the house and found the people at the gate, enjoying that last and sweetest conversation of the doorstep.

Helen and George determined to go home by train, so they walked on to Putney Bridge Station. They naturally did not talk of the meeting; it had been too obviously an experiment to allow them to begin at once discussing it; but when they got out at

Earl's Court, and were walking down the road, she began—

"It wasn't quite satisfactory. I'm sure you think so?"

"Yes, there was something wrong about them. What struck me was that there's still the trail of art about these people, and their socialism is so theoretical and unreal."

Directly he had said this, it seemed to her that she had known it all the time. That was what she thought.

He went on—

"Their position is like their house and its surroundings—at least, so it strikes me. Don't you know, a pretty, quiet house, built in perfect taste, furnished, not with old things, but with new things somewhat on an old model; things made now, but a little out of the natural course. And this house is surrounded by a multitude of little, bright, red-brick houses—absolutely vile and tasteless. And yet these new little houses are an attempt to carry out as much of the Withers' school of taste as is feasible I mean that these new little streets are what the common world makes of the Withers' artistic movement. And then even the Vineyard doesn't quite stand on all fours with itself. Outside it's white and elegant, with green painted woodwork round the windows—I think there are even green persiennes. Inside you would expect polished floors, a French style of furniture, polished. But when you go inside, and it's all filled with rawness. Raw terra-cotta colours, raw boards, raw carpets, and raw chairs. A rawness not of primitive times, but of a civilisation that has returned from polish. They've gone one better than elegance."

She laughed at his exposition. As they were turning out of Abingdon Road into Wright's Lane, Helen told him that they would be going away almost directly. Her mother was much better, and the doctor wished her to start for the east coast before it grew too cold.

VI.

THE next day, when George came home in the afternoon, he found a letter from Helen, saying that her mother had decided to go at once; they were starting that afternoon at four o'clock. The note ended with their address at Cromer.

Immediately George had read Helen's letter he sat down to write an answer —he felt the need of speaking to her at once, she meant everything to him now. He wrote warmly and enthusiastically, telling how much he owed her and how great a difference she had made in his life. Now that she was by him, or the thought of her, he could bear anything; for he could always be sure that with her he had all that was necessary, a continual and full contentment. Nothing would matter much now. When he read over his letter again, he felt doubtful. As long as they had been actually together there was no doubt, his behaviour was simple, their companionship frank and unmistakeable; but a littler was different; she was not there to give him the tone and to make him feel safe. He could imagine the letter not reading well. He conquered his doubt, and overcame the difficulty by openly stating it to her.

"Although I know you are safe there, and still really a near companion, yet I miss your actual presence, as perhaps you will see by this letter, which I am writing at once in my eagerness to be with you. So if there is anything amiss with the letter, and I feel doubtful about it, you will generously understand it, not think it ridiculous or beyond the mark."

George had been writing to his mother regularly once a week; but he had found little to say in his letters. He told her at first that it was lonely in empty London, he told her of the visits to Miss Spencer, to Mrs. Lemardelay and Iseult Withers; but he told her only the facts. His mother knew nothing of his troubles and trials, and he would have to begin so far back in order to explain. And even if he could make everything clear, she would think it was only imagination and waywardness, because she had not noticed the real meaning of it herself. And without this impossible explanation his sudden great companionship with Helen would be inexplicable. There in a man's falling in love with Helen Lemardelay—even at first sight—nor in a girl's inclination for George. But a companionship, a sudden and complete intimacy, the perfection of contentment following upon it, and never a word of love spoken—that was a different thing. Besides, it was their own affair, and why should he trouble to explain?

He got a letter back from Helen. It was short, but reassuring. She begged him to write often, always: and to say everything without fear, it was a joy for her to read what he wished her to hear. She wrote nothing about Cromer in her letter. Except for the postmark on the envelope and the address at the top of the sheet, she might just as well have been in London.

In his third letter to her he wrote that he had been to the Withers'. He felt the same about them; but they had all been very kind to him, and they were nice people. They talked shop perhaps a little too much, were a little too pleased at being together. He had been reading accounts in the paper of the threatened strike, and with his head full of realities he had said something about being abstract and ineffectual to the Cambridge man, for he was still rather expected to talk as an enemy. The answer was—

"We are the head, the brain of socialist movement. Somebody must do the abstract reasoning, others apply principles to actual facts. One man can't do everything, and the brain is as useful as the hand."

Some ten days after they had parted, he wrote that he was going to hear John Fisher speak in Islington, and that he had great hopes of finding him splendid; he had heard so much about him, and he was not an abstract socialist, having been trained in practice all his life as secretary of great unions, and he was said to be more thoroughly trusted by workers than any one else.

On that Saturday George made his way out to Islington, found the hall, and took his seat in the front. It was empty when he came; but after a few minutes he heard the sound of a band. People began to arrive in numbers, and the hall filled fast. The men came in laughing and joking, talking over the procession which had marched through the streets on its way to the meeting. Some in the front benches stood up and turned round, calling to friends whom they saw at the back; every one began to close up so as to make room. The band came in, and with them the builders' banner. All around him George heard the men who were quite at home critically considering the procession and meeting. The hall was often used by the Salvation Army. "Hallelujah" and "Welcome" hung in red cloth across the platform, with the name of the manufacturer written large in the corner; and the walls were covered with questions such as—"Where will you spend Eternity?"

After the band had played some popular songs for five or ten minutes, the chairman got up and introduced the first speaker. He was rather dull, and he often muddled himself by the use of parliamentary phrases and little roundabout introductions. The next speaker was interesting; he talked, perhaps, too much about the work which he himself had done when secretary of a union; but he was enthusiastic.

At last the speaker of the afternoon got up amid loud cheers. He was a dark man with a strong face, well dressed. From the very first words which he said until the end George was wrapt in admiration. The man spoke for over half an hour without a note, without a single hesitation, a logical, well-argued speech. He used a delightfully comprehensive and homely wit—people's wit, and the audience shouted with laughter. The next moment he was passionate, grinding out a sentence with a perfect use of his voice and gestures; but never rambling or losing the thread of argument. His great idea was the necessity of working so-operation together with trades' unionism. The one must help the other: if they were both properly developed, things would go smoothly.

George had a delightful vision of the House of Commons dwindling down to a kind of Oxford Union Debating Society. As it was, they spent weeks and weeks over nothing at all, whereas one man like this was starting a work which was likely to develope co-operation and trades' unions into the practical government of the country upon all the really important questions. This idea delighted George, for he hated politics. Here was something tremendous in import to the country, which was going to disregard politics.

"Take whatever either political party will give you," the speaker said, "but don't trust to either. You can get on quite well without them." Co-operation and trades' unions properly developed made socialism no longer a Utopian dream—a hard and fast system to be suddenly put into action—but a legitimate growth, something which was practicable because it had come gradually. And this socialism was the work of all these thousands of men, the real strength and citizenship of the country, who cared not a jot for Home Rule, Disestablishment, or even for an Eight Hours Bill. It was not only possible to become enthusiastic and sympathetic with these men, it was unavoidable. How was it that he had never seen this before? How could he have been so egotistical as to be melancholy when all this was going on? And he pictured himself some months ago at a meeting of this kind. He would probably have tried to keep up his artistic vision, even if he had felt inclined to give way. He would have dwelt upon his ambition of the speakers, on the enthusiasm carrying away a mass of men—all the old humbug. No, it was worse than humbug. It was disgusting, almost blasphemous, to be still concerned with such shams and educated theories in the face of all this humanity and real need. How much he owed to Helen! How he would work at this, carrying out the broader part of her gospel of sympathy.

John Fisher ended with a magnificent peroration, in which he placed all his theories and demands on an ethical basis. George felt that quite a little time ago he would have scoffed at this, even if he had been enthusiastic over the theories. "We are becoming strong, we will have out turn, if we can," would have been enough for him. But this man was saying that it was not enough, that he believed in a higher sanction—and now George sympathised entirely.

He left the hall immensely excited, joining in with the remarks and the praises of the men around him. When he came home, he sat down and wrote to Helen, his mind full of the new life he had gained from that evening's meeting, and looking forward hopefully to work in the future.

This letter was almost as great a delight to Helen as George's presence had been.

He had started on the new line, and she had begun her new life; here was a clearer proof than anything before. It was so good that he by himself had been carried away by this movement, that he understood it so fully, that it agreed so well with his inmost feelings. The letter in which she answered him was in a new strain. He had grasped the principles and was already beyond her. Her letter showed a caressing affection which she would hardly have expressed to him if they had been together, but which came naturally now that he had done so well. So completely had the enthusiasm taken hold of him that, as he owed to her, he had felt ashamed of himself when the resolution was put at the end of the meeting. The chairman had read from a paper something to the effect that all should join their union and do everything in their power to strengthen it; and he had hardly felt justified in holding up his hand for the "ayes."

She told him how much this new enthusiasm meant to her too. She also had been greatly in want of something; sometimes she called it freedom, sometimes an occupation. It was curious that freedom and a complete occupation had been one and the same thing in her mind. The want had continued to be vague, and she only understood its intensity now that she saw clearly that its satisfaction lay in this new thing which they had struck out between them. So much she told him. Her mind was ceasing to distinguish this new salvation from the personality of George, and this tenderness and respect for him showed itself here and there in the letter. He stretched himself back in his chair with a shudder of ecstasy as he saw through the letter Helen sitting at the table away in Cromer; one hand, and he saw its shape and colour, holding the note-paper, willingly resting upon what was to be his, her right hand penning the words, her face close above with a smile on the lips and her eyes thinking of him.

September was already advanced—the schools had begun. People were coming back to town, talking of their holidays, and very well pleased with themselves, bumptiously healthy, full of rather noisy and disturbing pity for those who had been left in London all the time. The man whose work George had been doing came back and took his place again. George had hoped at first that he should be able to stay on; but none of the staff were leaving, and he had not shown himself so brilliantly useful as to make them wish to keep him on unnecessarily. He felt that he had missed his chance. He did not express particular annoyance when he wrote of this to Helen. He only regretted that he as yet knew too little of trades' unions, strikes, and socialism to write about such subjects. In any case, the paper on which he had worked was not at all likely to want a socialist member on the staff. There must be a time of waiting and study. Some reviews, an article now and then could be written for the paper. Meanwhile he must work hard and learn as much as he could. He would understand all social questions, and keep abreast with the development of strikes, trades' unions, co- operation. He would catch up the Withers' school; he would get a grasp on socialism in Germany. But not only that. He would study such things as Toynbee Hall and the People's Palace, charities, the Salvation Army social wing. Nothing should be left dark to him in all this region.

Full of hope and strength he looked forward and considered these things. And, like a stranger, his vision fell on his old hopes. No wonder he had despaired! When he was still in the misty stages, before he had tried and found what reality meant, he had dreamt of two studies which were to fill in the hours when his stories flagged. One was a comparative history of the Romantic movement of 1830 in England, France, Russia, and Germany. He still had some notes which he had written on the subject. Another was to be a monumental book, the history of Venus from the earliest times, through the Greek stages, through Rome into the Middle Ages up to the Venusberg and Botticelli. What illustrations there would be, and what magnificent lines to quote. Especially the Venus of the Middle Ages, that was to be a joy. And then, what a chance for an exquisite piece of writing to explain why the book stopped at Botticelli.

Yes; no wonder he had despaired! No wonder he longed for something more human and nearer life, something broader and stronger, not so refined and studious.

George told his mother that he no longer had a place on the paper. He had given her hopes that the holiday engagement would be permanent. Still she would not have blamed him if he had merely stated the fact that he was no wanted. But in his inexperience he went further and told her part of the truth. He said that he did not much mind, he had not tried very hard, his heart was not in the work, and now he was going to try something different. He showed her some of his enthusiasm. His mother was swayed by the justifiable parental fear of any occupation which is entered upon with enthusiasm. Write poetry, music—do anything; even paint if you like; only not if your heart is in it. The change in George made a breach between mother and son. And although he assured her that there was practical use in learning about strikes and co-operation, that they were material for articles, still, remembering the enthusiasm, she was tormented by the fear that instead of being in a respectable position and able to marry, he would waste all his energies over a fad.

However, after the first disappointment and shock at hearing her son's partial confession, the matter did not appear so bad. He had got work sooner than had been expected; and now, although not in any post, he seemed to be fully occupied with this study, which, after all, was perhaps useful to a journalist, as it was evidently the question of the day.

The sudden change and enlightenment which had come upon George, and the particular inspiration of Fisher's meeting, found an expression in an article which he wrote at the end of the third week in September. It was a renunciation of art. Art is well in itself, but the time for it is over now. There will no doubt come a time when art is once more a worthy occupation. But now it is not the concern of the day and therefore it is false and selfish.

He had never done anything so good; the eloquence of the article, the conviction with which it was written, struck even the writer himself with astonishment. It really was rather a grand piece of writing, full of fervour caught from the bitterness of his own short experience—an appeal to his contemporaries to weigh his arguments and no longer to depend despairingly on the hopeless cause of art. Art could not mean a full occupation, an energetic life to such as they: it had been, and it would be; but it was not then. Social questions, in the broadest sense, were now the fit study of the young generation. The idle, the discontented, the blasé, would find enthusiasm and vigour there and only there.

VII.

THE article appeared in a socialist journal belonging to the Withers, rather a dilettante paper; however, the appeal was not to the workers, but to the others. He sent it to Helen just two days before she left Cromer. She did not write and thank him, but she said in a note, "Come for me at three the day after to-morrow to Wright's Lane."

She behaved much as usual to her mother in the train on the way back, perhaps speaking a little less. But her thoughts were fixed upon George—as they had been during the whole visit to Cromer—only with a new intensity which had been awakened in her by his article, the letter which had accompanied it, and the thought of meeting him again. The intensity was immeasurable, she had never imagined that there would be anything so profound. They arrived at King's Cross a little after two o'clock. She could talk and think no longer; she sat, her mind a blank, simply waiting. She was tired out into being merely the absolute expectancy, waiting personified.

It was three o'clock before they turned into Wright's Lane. George was standing near the gate with his back turned. At the sound of wheels he faced round, and in a second the carriage was at the door. Mrs. Lemardelay shook hands with George; Helen did not seem to want to begin looking at him and greeting him yet. Her mother was too tired to notice George much; she said to her daughter—

"Helen, I think I'll go upstairs at once and lie down. You must be very tired too, won't you follow my example?"

"No thanks, mother, Mr. Aston and I will have a stroll together."

"What, directly?"

It seemed a mad thing to Mrs. Lemardelay; but she spoke no more. Helen said to George, almost without looking at him—

"Will you wait a moment or two for me, do you mind?"

She went upstairs, took off her cloak, and washed her hands and face and was down at his side again. They went out of the house door, along the short path and through the gate into the street. The first words he spoke to her were—

"You're sure you're not tired?"

He might have said this to a stranger, he knew that she was not tired, and yet it seemed the fitting thing to say.

They had gone a few steps up the High Street when he noticed that her ungloved hand was hanging at her side close to his. He remembered how he had looked longingly at that hand nearly a month ago, when Helen stretched it out upon the table at her side as a preface to her invitation for that Saturday evening. She seemed to know what was in his mind, for she moved it nearer his. Their hands closed into one another—she had so much to tell him.

And they walked holding hands up High Street. "Dear Kensington!" as they both said hand in hand among the people.

"We neither of us thought of going into the garden, did we?" Helen asked.

"No." It seemed much better to be journeying close together out among people than to be in the garden, walking round and round. The made their way along side by side, unobservant, as children are unobservant. Everything was easy, as it is easy to an unconcerned child. George felt as if his eyes were very wide open and had returned to their childish gaze. They were silent, except for the few words which Helen spoke now and again;

and they were more like snatches of an unknown song which a baby croons to itself, wandering about in a wood through the tall grass, now standing to wonder at a butterfly, now bending down to a flower.

They went into the Gardens, not at a corner, but at the gate opposite De Vere Street. When they came to the grass stretch at the back of the Flower walk, they sat down. So long as they were moving, they had held hands as comrades; but when they sat down it was different, they naturally let go.

And then they began to talk. They had not spoken till then, not knowing where to begin in their wish to say the most important thing first, and fully; but they had said all that during their silent walk.

They talked on, Helen thanking George for his article, George telling her again how great the meeting was. And such conversation mingled with delicious irruptions of personal matters—

"Your mother must have thought it very strange of you to start out for a walk at once."

"I daresay it did seem childish. But I couldn't bear to think of anything coming in between my arrival in London and my talk to you. It would have made me miserable to have eaten meals, gone about the house, unpacked, and perhaps gone to bed before I could tell you, fresh from my eagerness in Cromer, everything I feel."

Then they would talk about the work which he meant to do—and that would be interrupted to say—

"How lovely it is to be together again"—with some fresh proof on her part of the absolute non- existence of the place Cromer in her mind during her mother's visit there. After they had sat a long time, they went on further, along the path which leads out into Lancaster Gate.

They went back the high road, and then home by Church Street. They did not reach Wright's Lane till nearly seven, and at the door she said—

"I'm growing so insatiable, so greedy! It's bad to have to part and to live through hours or a day alone. Greed it is, for if I'd been told months ago that I should have one hour a week of companionship like this I should have said that it would satisfy me."

The next afternoon at six o'clock George was returning home from his usual walk between tea and dinner. He had been in the Brompton Road, and he was coming back by Nevern Square. London was in one of its best moods. The evening sunlight of September was not so pale as it had been in the day, and very soft; there had been a little rain some hours before, and the leaves of the trees overhanding the road were glistening. The boys and girls in the Square had fallen back into their old July plan of playing a kind of cricket to finish up the day. It was still summer and they could still do it. When they had finished tennis, before they went in, one would stand in the corner, a friend would bowl for him and he would hit the ball out into the field to be caught by any one among the rest who were scattered over the lawn. This game was immensely enjoyed, and was an honoured custom. It entailed much joking and shouting, and the shrill screams of the girls sounded high above the laughter. At the top of the Square two cabbies seated on their hansoms turned in opposite directions were lazily chatting. A parlour-maid was talking out of the dining-room window to a man at the area railings.

On the opposite side of the Square, in front of him, George's eye was caught by the figure of a girl standing on the balcony. He recognised the figure and the dress—a stiff, dark-blue linen

jacket and skirt, quite plain. The girl was standing looking side-
ways down the street at a little group of children surround-
ing an organ-grinder and his monkey. Everything was soft and
friendly, Londoners were playing at summer for the last few days
as they used before they went to the country. As George walked
slowly on, nearer to the girl in the balcony, she moved her head
and recognised him. She turned back, leaning inwards, her right
hand resting on the rail, her left raised and touching the side of
the open window. She called into the room. Another figure appeared in the window and stepped out to the balcony. Helen put
her arm round her waist, and, leaning over the rail, she pointed
down to the man standing below in the street.

Helen made no sign to George, Margaret did not speak; but
the two girls, with their arms round each other's waists, leant
upon the rail and looked over at him.

Helen could not have called to him then, she had no wish
to run down and speak to him; but she felt a joy in standing up
there, safe, holding Margaret at her side, and looking down
smilingly. It was a kind of primeval feeling, something like a sav-
age and her love—as primeval as when they walked hand in
hand along the High Street.

George passed on. He did not know the house. Probably
Mrs. Forde was living there for the time, and Margaret and Hel-
en were spending the evening with her—he knew that Margaret
had been staying at the house in Campden Hill since her return
from Dieppe.

The next day was Sunday, Miss Spencer's day, the first after
the summer holidays, so that there was a great gathering at her
house. Henry Bishop was there with his sister. George had not
seen him since he went to Dieppe, for he had not made haste
to call on his old college friend as he would else probably have
done—he felt so far away from him now. Henry knew nothing
about the great change which his friend had undergone. He had

shared in his melancholy while at college, but somewhat cheer-fully. Naturally George did not say anything about what had happened, because where was he to begin? Henry was looking very interesting, talking enthusiastically about Ibsen to two sisters.

Mrs. Lemardelay was sitting on a bench near the balcony steps with Miss Spencer, who got up every now and then to receive the visitors announced from the drawing-room, and Mr. Withers, the father, was with them. At the end of the garden George joined a group of ladies—Helen, Margaret, Mrs. Forde, Iseult. As he walked towards them Helen came forward to meet him, Margaret stood by, with a smile on her face; she and the other two ladies shook hands warmly with him—he had seen them so often before, here and elsewhere, as a mere acquaintance.

"Would you take us to have some tea, Mr. Aston?" Helen asked.

They all moved off together towards the house, and stood by the table which was placed upon the gravel path under the drawing-room; they drank their tea and chatted, George hand-ing them their cups all round.

Mrs. Lemardelay in a few minutes rose from her seat, shook hands with George, and said to Helen—

"I think I must be going. Will you come too, or will you stay a little longer?"

"Oh, I think I'll stay, mother."

Mrs. Lemardelay went back to the seat to say good-bye to Miss Spencer. Mr. Withers, still sitting on the bench , asked—

"Who's that young man with Helen and Iseult? Is that Aston?"

"Yes."

"Oh, then it's he who has led Helen astray? I heard they had gone to one of Iseult's meetings."

"Yes, they like each other's company apparently."

"Why do you allow such things to go on?"

Mrs. Lemardelay raised her eyebrows slightly, gave the faintest approach to a shrug of her shoulders, smiled, said good-bye to Miss Spencer, and went off through the drawing-room.

Miss Spender had gone away, and Mr. Withers was left sitting alone, with his legs stretched out and his hands in his pockets defiantly, while the group of tea-drinkers chatted on near him.

Helen and George strolled about together and talked to Henry Bishop, who had a volume of stories coming out at the beginning of the next month. His sister Henrietta was standing by, glad to be out, and yet a little irritable and discontented. She looked pretty, very much one of a large number of girls who all look alike, all tall, well groomed, dressed fashionably, with somewhat expressionless faces.

George walked home with Helen. She had fully made up to him for her behaviour on former occasions when he had met her in society. Something of this kind was in her mind, for she said—

"You see how they are all much like other people when you know them, aren't they?"

When they came to her house she said, "Won't you come in a minute?" and immediately went on as if something were on her mind, "I somehow felt sorry afterwards that I should have let you pass on yesterday without speaking to you—I don't know exactly why I did it."

They had reached the drawing-room by this time and found it empty. George would hardly have come in with her if she had not begun making excuses directly after giving her invitation. They talked on for a little.

When he got up to go she put both her hands in his and smilingly lifted her face for him to kiss.

It was the first time, and there was nothing which George could have seen to lead to it at this particular moment. But Helen was thinking of yesterday evening a little sorrowfully, and of how gently he had always behaved, particularly this afternoon when she had made him happy by staying with him right through the visit to Miss Spencer.

[A note: Because of an editing error in the original, the text as published lacks a Chapter VIII.]

IX.

HELEN LEMARDELAY and George Aston were married half-way through November. Nothing and no one stood in their way. Helen had some eight hundred pounds a year of her own, part of some money which her father had inherited from a brother. George's position, which might have seemed an objection to those who did not know them, only added to her desire for the marriage. He would not long be able to continue without an occupation, giving up his time to the new work. But on her money they could both live, and he would be able to spend his whole time in learning all he wished, and then he might get work on some paper which devoted much space to the labour question. He was to become a great authority.

Some of their less intimate friends thought that the marriage was hasty. But they did not know how completely they filled up each other's needs, and how strong the needs in these young people had been—and there was no reason for waiting. The lease of the house in Wright's Lane, too, was falling in at Christmas, and Helen could not think of beginning another chapter of life still living with her mother. Mrs. Lemardelay was taking a flat at the other end of the High Street, opposite the entrance to the Gardens.

Helen and George went north for their honeymoon. They felt now as they felt that first afternoon when she returned from Cromer, not the least desire to run away and hide their joy and be alone. They wished to enjoy the charm of being together and belonging to each other in the midst of the world and its work. They therefore went north and visited the towns concerned in the great strike which had been threatening so long, and had broken out at last. That remained to her till the end of her life, the wonderful impression of the delights of their honeymoon in the midst of the enormously important movement. That time was not a dream of joy, as she had read in books. It was an awakening. Her past life was the dream; now she had found out what life really was. There was this wonderful combination of love with work to be done together. Their honeymoon was a fit overture to the harmony of life which she had discovered when she met George.

As for Mrs. Aston, the marriage was the last step in the course which had bit by bit separated George from his mother. He was now free; he depended upon her for nothing. And she was jealous, not so much of the love between George and Helen, as of the new power of this other person, who could give her son as much as she herself could offer, and more. George had not become possessed of his independence by any effort of his own. Then she would have been proud. No, it was rather as if he had chosen another mother. They had grown apart, as the two generations always do, and now that Helen held out her hand, offered more than she could, he separated from her gaily. She was nothing to him, he could do with her, and she came to think that she had never been really anything in his heart. Mrs. Lemardelay she had seen a few times and did not like, but for Helen she had always had a fancy, so that there was no dislike in the case. It was simply a fresh person sailing upon the scene, do-ing nothing and capturing her son, eclipsing a long twenty-three years of devotion. She had been vexed that her son had changed his plans and become socialist. Yet that vexation was better than this entire severance.

When they came back at Christmas time Mr. and Mrs. George Aston took furnished lodgings because they did not wish to be hampered with a house. They would go from place to place, according to circumstances. An arrangement of this kind, as everything else which they did, seemed to come from both husband and wife at the same time; no completer unity could be imagined.

One of the first things which they did was to go to Kensington and look at the old house. As they came in sight of the well-known stretch of wall on the right-hand side of Wright's Lane they walked more slowly. There was something forlorn and faded about it. The time when they had been together there seemed to have been long, long ago. They saw the old place, sleeping, empty, and peaceful, and were astonished, as people always are in such cases, that it was still the same. It looked to them desolate on this cold winter's morning, because they knew it was empty; but people were passing along the High Street, and many were turning the corner, bright and cheerful, not noticing the empty house. Helen and George were not saddened. They had left the old times far behind, and were with the busy passers-by concerned in their engrossing affairs. There was a board up announcing that the house and land were to let.

They went up the High Street, for they were to lunch with Mrs. Lemardelay. She lived in a flat in a huge red-brick building, which had only been finished a few months. It was the work of one of the younger members of the school, who had turned architect. The gentle quietness and old-fashioned air of the old house, and its big pleasant garden, with the seat round the cedar-tree, shut in from the world by high walls, only admitting a few select artistic people, was left for the third floor of a bright, red- brick mountain with a lift; the roar of the street mounts up into the rooms. But the lift has little pieces of wrought-iron fixed about it, and the incandescent lamps are curved and prickly. The windows are of bottle-glass or else hung with bead blinds, and there are still the sketched of the master hanging in the drawing-room.

During the strike George had been irritated by the way in which some newspapers had taken hold of certain mistakes made by the leaders of the strike, and had lost sight of the great principle concerned, preaching, perhaps, some rather shaky political economy. Their coldness and want of brotherly feeling, even if they thought that the strikers were wrong, astonished

George and made him indignant. A very elementary indignation. He was shocked that people who at any rate lived com-
fortably should be so hostile to thousands of their fellow-men
in worse circumstances. Suppose they were wrong, was that a
reason for being unbrotherly?

At this moment both Helen and George were beginning their
study of charities. This was part of their scheme; part of the
gospel of the time which they had discovered. George had no
great faith in charity, but he would gain if he confirmed his prej-
udice, because he could then depend entirely on the other side
of social work.

A life of committees and discussions began. For months they
worked together, taking a personal delight in the communion
of thought and labour, even if in itself the thing studied gave
less satisfaction. Helen would always be on in front, a pioneer,
discovering new phases. George would follow, take up what she
had discovered, and form an opinion upon it. She would move
on uncritically, showing one new thing after another; he would
comprehend and criticise, carrying her absolutely with him in
his judgment. And so they lived in perfect unity, going about
together, each with an especial province: the woman, with her
quickness, in front, turning up the sand which contained the
jewels, and looking back with love into the eyes of the man for
whose sake alone she worked; and the man following in her
steps, looking closely, choosing critically and slowly among the
treasures which lay along the stretch chosen out by her quick
sense.

They loved the sympathy, and on they worked; but his prej-
udice against charities was confirmed, and she agreed. There
was nothing grand or beautiful about charities as far as he could
see. The old charity—yes, there was beauty in that—the beggar
moving the rich man to pity by his appeal. That was personal;
there was a kind of feudal air about such charity; something that
brought with it vague remembrances of pilgrims, castles, saints,

and apparitions of Christ; but this new charity, impersonal and organised, with officers who distribute what the rich give thoughtlessly in order to get the poor off their minds and out of their sight, was mistaken. The other was natural; it was the appeal of one man to another against fate's decree; the rich was moved with pity and gave. The old feudal charity, though pretty, was probably impossible now; but that did not prove the other to be right.

It was a mistake and no progress could be expected from it. It was all part of the false system by which the rich pay for the policemen to keep the criminals out of their way, and pay for prisons in which to hide them, whereas it seemed that if a person lived in a society he should bear to the full the difficulties to which it gave rise. The whole society is liable if one is a criminal; and if there are to be prisons, every one should take their turn of hard labour.

And from charities they went on to the next step, Helen throwing herself hopefully into the region of societies for the improvement of the poor. Here, at least, people worked personally. Helen and George became acquainted with believers in temperance, in missions, in Toynbee Hall, the People's Palace, and boys' and girls' clubs. Helen worked hard and George did a good deal. It was said that by these means, at any rate, a man might become acquainted with the poor and their needs. The inseparable couple came to be well known among clubs and organisations in all parts of London; no one dreamt of mentioning them apart. Helen and George worked absolutely together. Neither had a thought of which the other did not know and when George fell out of sympathy, as he had done before, they were still together.

One or two striking pictures and situations had crystallised George's vague misgivings. One Saturday evening he was in the Mile End Road, sharing in the enjoyment of the parade, the booths, the movement, the lights, the free laughter and chaff.

The whole place was full of life, and there was an air of simple gaiety which was almost continental, an enjoyment of nothing at all. At one time the whole street seemed to be chanting the latest popular song. The entrance to the Paragon looked bright. Those who had six-pences to spare and had gone in with their wives and children to spend a pleasant evening, and to refresh their recollection of the great comic singer who had taken their world by storm. Helen walked at his side, enjoying the company and his enjoyment. Suddenly the pleasant light of gas and petroleum flares was interrupted by the cold, desolating electric light. An enormous building without a front rose into view. It was the People's Palace. Joy stopped there. They passed through the solitary turnstile, and the railings covered with boards announcing shorthand and French lessons, into an immense forsaken hall, lit by electric light, and containing some plants in pots. There were three people in it; an old man and an old woman with a little girl.

Or, again, he went to a meeting of a University society for the improvement of the people in Whitechapel. A Cambridge secretary spoke about their work. They were teaching people how to enjoy themselves rationally, giving them books, lectures, debating clubs, gymnasiums. And George had a vision of the heavy boredom of the upper-class Englishman, of the extreme difficulty which he finds in amusing himself, and passing his leisure hours. While, in the streets, a promenade, a song, laughter, was enough. And to see the girls dancing to an organ, and a ring of people watching! The working man who spoke at the meeting, although he meant to be favourable, made such a much better speech than the Cambridge secretary, and touched upon so many points which told both ways, or even were adverse to the improvers, that he was, to George's mind, pleading against them.

So they went on month after month, charmed to be working together, becoming intimate with that large circle of people whose minds are completely filled with thoughts of social improvement—finding a sufficient employment in their discovery that those people were unsympathetic.

The various makeshifts with which Society tried to blind itself to the necessity of socialism were criticised, and the steps in the process were marked by articles in different papers, but mostly in the Withers' journal. For during all this time, though he did not lose his original unfavourable impression, he had remained on good terms with the artistic socialists, and continued to attend their meetings. And after two years of experiment, during which he gradually gave up his connection with philanthropy, he found himself closer to the Withers school than to any other. But, as time went one, a new difficulty began.

He had objected openly to some of their ways, and had even written for their paper a warning against the dangers of abstract socialism, of theories which only serve to divide. They accepted such criticism as natural and fair, and the article came well in the paper, as it was not an attack, but a warning from their own side.

But during February in the third year of their marriage, when he had less to occupy his thoughts than usual, he found that instead of combating those of their opinions which he disliked, he was unconsciously noticing and collecting little points about the whole set which joined themselves together into an extremely ridiculous sketch. They were little things which he said to Helen about them, and over which she laughed, though they were not at all when she herself would have noticed. One day in the early spring, when the completeness of the sketch was irresistibly tempting, he began writing. And some days after, what he had written seemed so good that he wondered whether he would send it to a paper. But then he thought it was rather unkind. Yet it was so comic. He showed it to Helen. She was astonished that George had cared to amuse himself thus, especially when he spoke of sending it to a paper.

"Why do you wish to do that?"

"I didn't think very seriously of doing so, perhaps I'd better not, because they mightn't like it; but it reads so funnily."

"Of course, I think it's amusing because I know the people; but do you think any one who didn't would?"

"Oh, there's no fear of people not understanding it. The thing is obvious enough."

"If you attacked their opinions, that would be all right. Write your article upon their mediaeval socialism."

"If I did that I should be much more violent, for I should be a partisan. I should be hard on them then; but in this case I'm not hostile; I'm not even laughing. I simply represent certain points."

"They certainly will be hurt by this much more than by an attack, because there's no answer. But I can't see why you wish to publish this; it comes to nothing."

"No; it's not worth while; it was only an idea."

Helen could not understand what he meant. The sketch certainly amused her, because she knew the people and recognised the descriptions of them and their houses; but it would not be anything for others. She was not so much concerned with the question of the feelings of her friends as with her own feeling that it was a piece of fooling unworthy of George. He had not enough to do at the time, and she was glad that in May they were to start for the Continent. He was to begin with Belgium, and write accounts to a morning paper of socialism there, then they were to go on to Germany. It was now just the turning-point; they had passed through the preliminary stages; they were going to start on real socialism. Meanwhile they were idle; he said that it was not worth while to begin anything in England. She urged him to write about mediaevalism, an attack which she knew would by violent. He wrote something, but did not publish it; he said he would wait.

X.

ON an afternoon, half way through September, George was sitting in his room after tea. Helen had gone out to see her mother, George was tired and not very well, so he had stayed at home. They had come back from Berlin the day before. George sat in a listless, melancholy mood; his state of mind reminded him of the days before he was married, when he had come home from the country and sat and felt miserable at the prospect of a Cambridge winter term, or, further back still, of a term at school.

London had always been cheerless, he remembered, on those days. Sometimes he had left his mother and his brothers behind; but even when they came with him it was melancholy. There was nothing worth looking forward to; then the actual dread of the journey to school or Cambridge, the station, the men with their Gladstone-bags, talking shop, men already in couples, friendly already, and he himself shrinking from them, keeping to himself, now hopeless at the prospect of the winter, now filled with poignant regret at the picture of the sunny holiday.

And always in those times, as far back as he could remember, his regrets would centre round one person or one spot.

As if the pain at leaving the holiday place had been too general, some one thing would arise in his mind to make the pain acute. Once it had been a girl to whom he had never spoken, and the girl in particular surroundings, coming out of her white house with its green shutters on the sunny quay.

Another time it was a little girl of eleven, who had put her arm in his and run about the garden with him. And once his regrets were inextricably mingled with the pathos of a novel which he had been reading, until the heroine became the centre of his pain.... It was a windy day; the house seemed sometimes to rise, sometimes to swell with the gusts.

It was ridiculous to be so sentimental, he would look forward cheerfully to his work. And he set himself to thinking of all he had to do. He had made a name as an authority on socialism; his articles were to be re-published; he was to be regularly on the staff of the morning paper for which he had written; he had been asked to give lectures and to speak at meetings; some of the secret prominent of the trades' union secretaries were his friends and took him into their confidence; in fact he was well started on the work....

The intention was good, but it was no use. In Berlin he had lived from hand to mouth, writing his articles and getting them over, and then enjoying the actual new things which he saw, without entering into himself and considering what he meant by it all. But now, when he was trying to look forward to the work which he had begun, he felt like a child with his mouth full, when half through chewing, without a feeling of sickness, quite involuntarily, the mouth suddenly opens wide—ah—with a closed feeling in the throat.

And it was no use trying to deceive himself into hopefulness, he was alone with himself. That was a strange sensation too. Never before had he experienced this feeling of having to depend entirely on himself. When he was a boy there had been hope, and he had justified in waiting for help from outside. He felt afraid, the gusts swelled, drops of rain swung about in the grey air; it was hopeless, and there was nothing to comfort him. Helen's entrance would have been an interruption.

He left thinking of the future, and dreamt of the time which he had passed in Berlin. It was almost painful to remember some bits—the bright Potsdamer Strasse with its brilliant white houses and lime trees, and especially some places just out of the town;

a sandy slope beyond Wedding, with purple flowers growing in the sheltered parts, and then Halensee, the long sandy stretches grown with purple grass and sorrel and evening primroses, and the pine woods dripping down to a little lake, and the bier-lo-kal at Hundukehle and St. Hubertus. Or else the more obvious corners of the town: the view of the Linden, lighted by electric light, seen through the curtained windows of the great room in the opera house, the touching statue of the great Frederic, with the stretch of trees behind him.

How happily he had lived there, and how bright everything he had lived there, and how bright everything had been! He had not troubled to look forward; he just did his work con-scientiously, and the rest of the time he was free to appreciate this new town, to be a sensitive observer of all the aspects which struck him. He had allowed no misgivings to trouble him, he had put all questions off till he should return to London, and fully oc-cupied himself in enjoying and comprehending the sentiment in the town. Yes, that had been his business—strangely engrossing, for what was it after all? And here again he had the curious feeling of having to deal with himself only; for though he had sometimes tried to explain it to Helen, this pleasure, whatever it was, had been all his own.

And then he thought, "I'm not well. This regret for Berlin is fantastic and only comes because I don't feel fit for effort and fresh work." And yet he had nothing to set against his present hopelessness and the long dreary prospect expect this past en-joyment; it certainly had been acute, and had a peculiar halo of glory around it.

"How early it grows dark now," he thought, and looked at his watch; it was seven o'clock; Helen ought to be in; and just at that moment he heard the key in the door.

She came into the room and saw George sitting as she had left him. Immediately her while concern was for him. She was so little herself that the irritating "What, still sitting here?" the cheerful expression of personal astonishment, never even entered her head. She came up to him, took the hand which he held out, and sat down beside him. Then she said—

"I'm sorry I've been away so long."

"Oh, I've been sitting here doing nothing. I feel idle. How is your mother?"

"She's very well.... On my way I went to see the house. It has been bought by the drapers at the corner, and they are rebuilding it. I couldn't get in by the big gate, it was boarded up; but I went into the garden by the builders' entrance at the side. The house and everything looked so strange; I had to look a long time before I saw that all the things were really just as they used to be. The sort of idea I had about the house isn't a bit like what it really is."

During dinner and afterwards, George was preoccupied and did not speak much. Helen said not a word about his silence, or about his being unwell. She was simply there, and his entirely. This attitude of complete love and self-oblivion was irresistible, and George felt forced to speak.

"I shall be all right to-morrow. Changes always do upset me. I don't know why I should feel low-spirited exactly. But I can't become hopeful by thinking over the work we are going to do. I've been trying to rouse myself, but all I do is to drop back into thinking how delicious it was in Berlin. It is dreary to come back again."

As he began, it all seemed natural. He was not very well, he had done a good deal of work in Berlin, and now he felt tired and a little hopeless; that was to be expected. A man cannot always feel certain and vigorous about a great work in which he is engaged. But "it is dreary to come back again;" that struck a short, painful note upon a chord somewhere hidden away in her heart.

She comforted him, and they talked on a little longer. But when he had gone to bed and she was sitting up alone, the painful note began again to sound and brought back his words, "It is dreary to come back again." And now that he was not with her, she thought over these words and the pain came out clear. How strange, she thought, that he should feel this private regret at leaving one place for another.

Such an idea—a thought apart from him—could never have occurred to her.

And George had said the words quite openly, without the least idea of what they meant to her. He felt dreary at coming back to London, and so he said it, and he did not see what he was saying. His confession about his work gave her no pain, yet that was what George might have fancied would distress her.

It was dreary for him to come back to London. She had no idea that such a thing could be. He had a pleasure apart, a source of sympathy outside. Her fears came first; but then she calmed them. She was exaggerating; he was not well. They would see, he would be well again soon. Bishop was coming to dine the next day to talk over business, and that might set him right.

Henry Bishop, just before Helen and George started for Berlin, had made a proposal to George to carry out their old college plan of starting a weekly paper. George was to take charge of politics, which would be socialist. Henry would write stories and criticisms; and other friends, among them a musical student with advanced views, had promised to help them. Bishop would put in some money which his father was willing to give him for this purpose, and Helen would do the same; she thought the idea excellent, it would give George a fresh interest in social work. They had discussed the matter in Berlin and had written to Henry to say that on consideration they approved. And on

the next evening he was to come and make more definite ar-
rangements.

Helen had invited Margaret, for she and Bishop liked each
other, and as George had so neglected his old college friend of
late, she wished to have a pleasant party. Margaret, too, she had
seldom seen since since her marriage. George and she had been
so wrapped up in each other and the work which they were
doing, so contented after their discontent and emptiness, that
they had not needed their old friends. And now George had
expressed a wish to go back again; he felt a longing to see Henry
and have one of the old talks with him.

The meeting was very friendly. Towards the end of dinner,
after much personal talk, Henry and George began to discuss
the paper excitedly, continually springing up from the consideration of details into lofty ideas about art, or the way in which
things were to be viewed and articles written. And the eager
conversation was sprinkled with jokes which moved to endless
laughter, jokes about the greatness of the paper, the name of the
articles, and what people would say and how they would hold up
their hands and shake their fists. They were like boys over it.

Helen was delighted to see George show so much interest
and hopefulness; and Margaret, interested, glad that her two
friends were going to do this work, with only just a vague con-
sciousness of astonishment floating through her mind now and
again when she thought of Helen attached to a boy who was so
eager and full of theories—only dim little astonishments as she
looked at Helen.

They had been to talk for five minutes about such an actual
subject as the printer, when George said—

"And I know the way to treat my subject now. Something
quite new and much more striking than the mere up-holding
of opinions. People have had enough of bare opinions, we must
give them depth and reality, light and shade, by representing

things rather more descriptively. I can do the more ordinary style for the old daily, but you shall have something more sympathetic and infinitely more real—and it will be of interest to everybody, not merely to specialists."

"Yes, that's a great thing. The articles, even on remote subjects, shall be interesting to every one. And we shall all be working together. There's a thread which joins us already, and it will grow stronger. There will be no contradictions in our paper. And yet it will be broad and sympathetic, not narrow, and incapable of enthusiasms."

They talked until it was time for Margaret to go—they could have talk for ever. Helen and George went out and accompanied the other two to Portland Road Station, where they took train for Notting Hill Gate, for Margaret was staying in Campden Hill.

George felt cheerful after this meeting with Henry and the discussion about the paper. He did not know why the idea should make him feel hopeful; but somewhere in the back of his mind hopes sprang up: there seemed to be possibilities in the paper and in the renewal of his intimacy with Henry.

XI.

THE paper appeared in November. George's first two articles were drawn from his recollections of what he had seen of
socialism in Belgium. As he had intended, he taught very little
in the articles, and endeavoured to draw striking pictures—to
record, with more latitude than he had given himself before, the
situations which had taken his fancy. For the third week he had
already written a finishing article upon Belgium. With the fourth
he meant to continue the series with Berlin.

He sat in the evening at his writing-table calling up to his
remembrance with growing pleasure various scenes which in
Berlin. His recollection centred round the pine-woods and the
restaurants to the west of the town. They had no sort of connection with socialism; yet they seemed to be the flower of his Berlin
recollections. For some reason one particular spot rested in his
mind with peculiar vividness, and slowly he traces again every
step which he had made on that evening.

He had been strolling alone the whole afternoon in the country, and at five o'clock he was returning east towards the town.
The country was absolutely still, the sun was hot, the crickets
and larks were mingling their notes. He had passed through a
tiny avenue of old and worn fruit-trees, when suddenly he heard
the noisy clang of a bell and found himself at the top of a broad
road which turned down towards some houses. There was no
transition that he could remember, he was astonished to find
himself at once among a crowd of people who were waiting
for the noisy-ringing steam-tram to come and take them up.
He could not think why there were so many people about, hol-
iday-makers.

Then he remember that it was Sunday; but what they doing out there? He followed the road among a stream of people and reached the bottom of the dip. On the left lay a lake among reeds, and on the right there was a little group of willows, and among them an entrance to a restaurants which was out of sight. But through the willows the flash of water caught his eye, and the sound of music was accompanied by the continuous roll and thud of skittles. Two laughing girls in light dresses were turning into the entrance arm-in-arm.

The sudden change from the hot, flat, and silent plain to this noisy, gay corner among the reeds and willows of a lake affected him. And the impression was heightened as he walled on. For he came to a cross-road in which were some shops and houses, some old and some newly built. And at the doors of the old houses peasants were standing listlessly, gazing with open mouths into the street; in the wine shop there was a noisy quarrel going on, and in the first floor of a little cottage a man and a woman were cursing and shouting one another down. The sudden change had impressed him, and each point as it presented itself found a sensitive record.

Down the road, past a house, three or four steps into a field, and all was perfect silence again. Before him lay the beginning of Berlin, the great mass of the Joachimsthal school. A new road had been begun and reached half say across; but the meadows on either side were untouched and full of wild flowers, especially grass of Parnassus. It was perfectly still.

He remembered that he had been so moved as to wish to go again and take Helen to show her, though he did not know what had made him cling so to the recollection of this spot. They went together, and took a long time in finding it. When he came he was impressed again, though in rather a different way. He could not explain what he felt to Helen. Since then he had not thought of the place particularly. He had not written of it in his articles, fir it had nothing to do with them. But now he could think of nothing else. Why had this one place come back to his mind with such a glamour round it?

Why now, when he was intending to write on the Berlin socialists? The feeling reminded him of a morning in his boyhood when he was staying in Dieppe for the summer holidays. He woke up knowing that it was Saturday, the day for a ball at the Casino. And he began thinking over his partners one by one. When he reached one particular girl, the picture of her touched him, and gave a peculiar softness to his feeling, as if something had happened between them. And yet she was not an especial favourite of his, he had never paid her particular attention. And then the recollection came vaguely, and like a faint scent through a mist, that the causeless phantasy of the night's dream had made the girl sweet and caressing to him, and that he had kissed her then.

What was it now? What had passed between him and Wilmersdorf that he could think of nothing else? And what was to be done? The whole of his strange, intimate joy in Berlin, and his regret at leaving it, hung now upon this place.

As he thought over the little street with itshouses, a tragedy grew to match the laughter and the music and the flash of the reedy lake; how, years before, Wilmersdorf had been a silent, tiny hamlet inhabited by market-gardeners and day labourers; close to Berlin, only six or seven miles from the Bröse, and yet it was seen by no one, for it was on no high road. As Berlin grew after the war, the shopkeepers and townspeople spread abroad every Sunday to find a bit of country, and Wilmersdorf was discovered. People came gradually more and more. The one old innkeeper, who used to work in his garden all day, and only come in at certain hours to give the well-known customers a drink of white beer, was called upon to supply the visitors. He gave up his gardening and made an attempt, envied by his friends. But he could not manage the work; he was bought out by a man from the town, and his young daughter, an ignorant country girl, was

kept on at a salary as a waitress. And from that, the gradual
ruin of the old life in the little hamlet, as the visitors and
their visitors and their demands increased, and the villagers let
off working in order to try and supply their wants: the men idle
and unsettled, the girls ruined, yet even so no success—disor-
der everywhere. And gradually the building of fine restaurants
by the side of the lake—the place becoming as he had seen it.
The drunkenness and quarrelling, the cursing at misfortune,
the idle gazing at the visitors on Sunday and the dreariness of
Monday, the complete wreck of the village. And the last picture.
A few years afterwards, and Wilmersdorf is as orderly as it was
thirty years back. All the original inhabitants have been scattered— some of the men are working on behalf of their enemy
the town, building the road which runs west from Berlin. The
Berliners are amused in organised pleasure-gardens. There is a
big ball-room, entrance one shilling, boxes extra, and everything
is as business-like as at a chantant in the Alexandrinen Strasse.

And behind the tragedy came into his mind the scene of it,
the lake with its three restaurants hidden among the trees, the
triumphant bell-clang of the steam-tram skimming along the
road from Berlin.

And as it all came before his eye, the whole picture, crowded
with interest, calling for him to take it, he felt all his vigour
streaming back upon him like a flood. Now he was eager once
more to live on.

He had found it, he had found it; he had found it; found
the one thing for which he had been dimly searching these last
months. It was the gleam of the ocean which he knew, which
was his, and from which he had been exiled so long, on his
march through a strange land.

XII.

"HAVE you written your fourth article yet; the beginning of Berlin?"

"Yes, I've finished it. I'll show it you. I never wrote anything so easily. I've only done the beginning; but enough for an article. It's about the place which I took you to see that hot afternoon, out beyond the big school. I couldn't explain to you quite why it interested me so, but you'll see now."

When Helen had read it she said—

"How strange! That's not at all the impression the place made on me."

"No? Well it's most certainly the impression it made on me— not that the truth matters one way or the other."

For the first time since they had met, Helen was out of touch, and naturally, for George was away to a region of which she had no knowledge. She felt immediately that they were not together.

"It's to be an example of the ruin of village- life of which people talk so much?" she went on.

"Yes, it's a picture of what happens. But I shall draw no moral, for there's none to be drawn."

"It will remain simply a picture?"

When the complete vision of Wilmersdorf's story came to him that evening, it was the discovery of something which he seemed to recognise as the object of his vague search. He did not inquire any further, or connect it at all with Helen. His whole state of mind, his idleness, the dead lack of energy which had been growing slowly upon him when he thought of his work, the curious love for Berlin, where he had lived thoughtlessly and enjoyed something new, the dreariness of coming back to London, where it would be necessary to have it out with himself, the circling of his imagination round and round a spot vaguely seen, and the final discovery of what it meant, all was so entirely his own concern that he did not think particularly of Helen; why should he? And he himself had inquired into it so little.

But directly he saw Helen reading what he had written he began to feel that his new departure did not concern himself alone, and when she had finished he was certain that her first movement had been unsympathetic. Without reflecting how entirely he had lived for himself lately, whereas, before, everything he had done and felt sprung from his companionship with Helen, without seeing how impossible it would be for her to understand at once what this opening Berlin article meant to him, he was a little hurt offended at her want of sympathy. He did not go further than a slight sensation of distrust. But when once an artist feels, or imagines, the slightest want of he increases his hostility, adding brick after brick, until the wall of separation grows impassable and sheer.

When George gave Helen his article to look at, she thought that it would be a continuation of his former work. She read it through and found nothing in it. It was taken from a source of which she had no knowledge. She only knew that whatever it was, it had not sprung into being and grown up with her help, she had no part in it. The only criticism which came into her head was that the description did not recall the place. And when he told her later that this kind of writing was the solution of his difficulties, and the meaning of his vague feelings in Berlin, her fears of the day after their return came upon her in force. They came on her in overwhelming force, so that she could not think clearly—simply minute passed of blind fear, so that she grew hot and cold, and the sweat stood on her forehead. It was like a child's nightmare; he had been away and was still away somewhere in the distance at a point which she could not reach, infatuated with something which was out of range.

But the next morning she came back from her first extreme fears. There was George at her side, and what was the nightmare which had frightened her?

Two weeks passed away. The house was very lively. Henry Bishop was always there, and he was an enthusiastic, generous person, full of admiration for George, and very eager about the paper. Others who were connected with them often came to the house, and they sat and talked and cheered each other on and joked. Everybody was occupied, and that made Helen feel all the more acutely the sudden change which had come for her. During every minute of the three years of her life with George she had been occupied, she had been working, for George had taken his full draught of sweet sympathy after long thirst. Every part of his life was hers, it was perfect employment.

Now she was idle. But only for a time, surely only for a time; the change had come upon her unawares; she had not imagined such a thing. But it was only a whim, George would come back again to the work. The work, the great, noble work, her gospel, the discovery which they had made together, their life.

And as the days passed on she came to look forward to a particular evening just before Christmas, for which they had a long-standing invitation from John Fisher. It was for a small private meeting, just the secretaries of some of the most important unions. The invitation was a great honour, and they had been delighted when Fisher spoke of it to them long before. It would be a kind of introduction into the real working socialism, the crowning of their efforts.

A few days before the fifteenth of December, the evening appointed, she spoke to George of their engagement. She had said nothing before, because he was occupied, and it was only as time went on that she began to feel fully how idle the change had left her, and to fear how it would end. So she spoke, hoping to get back to their life together.

George, to her astonishment, said he could not go. She had not expected that.

"Really? You mean really that you don't wish to go?"

"I don't see how I can. The fifteenth is just the evening on which we meet to discuss the following number."

"But surely another day would do as well for that."

"No. It's most important that we shouldn't miss the meeting in which we arrange everything."

"Then you really don't wish to go?"

George was astonished now. Astonished at himself, astonished to think how entirely he had neglected her during these weeks. The tone of her voice discovered this to him. They had talked and laughed together with the rest, but he had not really thought of her. This feeling put him in the wrong, and Helen hurried on to speak, hating to see at a disadvantage, and sacrificing herself.

"Are you going to give up the work for the sale of this paper?"

"It's not so much for the paper as the work which I'm doing for it."

"But it is worth while, George, to give up such an important thing for such a slight one? You may miss your chance. You have full success in your grasp. You've gone through all the preliminaries, and now that you've reached the point for which you've been working, will you turn back just when you should go on, and for a fancy, a fancy which has taken you because you were tired and a little hopeless? Won't you begin again?"

"Helen, let us wait—let me wait a little and see," and he wanted to turn and speak of something different, to leave this untouched, and talk as people do usually, about anything.

Before they had gone abroad Helen had a vague fear for a short space. George might lose interest in the work for a time, and then the weight of bringing him back would rest with her. Something had made her look forward down the long vista of life and she thought she saw the possibility. But the fear had passed away. Now this was worse. He had gone away, and of his own accord, to something else, just when he had reached the important point. And she saw that he did not wish to say anything to her about this work, that he was making a division between it and his conversation with her, cutting her off from the one great interest which occupied his thoughts.

One day during the week she was alone with Bishop, and she said—

"George isn't going to write any more articles on socialism then, for I see you've got some one else to do them?"

"Yes, a man called Player. It's just as well to keep them on, because socialism is a thing of the time, and it would be a pity to miss the chance of sympathising with something important."

Henry knew nothing of what Helen and George had done together. He had begun again with his friend where he left off, taking the three years of estrangement as natural: "that's always what happens when people marry." And he was much too enthusiastic and concerned with art and ideas to notice anything now; indeed, that would have been difficult.

"I'm glad that George isn't doing them any more. He's writing excellent things now. That

Wilmersdorf sketch was wonderful; it took us all by storm. And now these character sketches which he's doing are delicious.

And I'm glad, too, that he's thinking of writing Wilmersdorf on a large scale, making a long book of it, and doing the town and the suburb and all the people thoroughly, like a Zola. It will be just as well, too, if he leaves off his work for the Chronicle. As he said, a man can't do two things at once, and he ought to give his whole time to this."

So it really was important as this? And they all knew about it. He had long plans in his head, and Bishop and the rest knew what was his intention.

And she felt as if she were drifting at sea. That of all things she could least bear. A safe anchorage, the feeling of certainty, or else a struggle against wind and tide—either of those suites her nature.

Meanwhile George was working hard, with all the vigour and hope which follows a fresh discovery. He was sweet and gay to Helen, always hoping that she would not go back to the serious subject; for he felt tender about her in this matter, and the thought of her disappointment now was a black shadow with his own invincible feeling of life and hope. He tried not to think of it, and to look forward and comfort himself with the idea that when his work became admired, everything would be right again; and his joy at his work was so great, it seemed to him impossible that the shadow could last.

Days passed away, and weeks. Helen went out very little. She felt always that George was afraid of talking to her about the change; she felt even how in his own mine he tried to put off thinking about it. She hoped that it was only a mood, and would pass; but fearful lest the separation between them should grow, she kept from talking to him about the one thing which she thought. She read the paper, paying no particular attention to his sketches, hardly knowing what they were about, simply waiting for the return. She knew nothing of what the world said of the paper, except what she had heard from the set who came to the house, and from them she gathered and vaguely understood that the world did not appreciate it. However, they made up for the world's unkindness by admiring each other.

Helen had taken Henry without criticising him, as a friend and admirer of George. But now she began to dislike him—this man who was in league with George, who knew all his plans, who raved over his work, and gaily les him on without noticing her. The one secret of George's which he did not know was the only thing in her life.

XIII.

A YEAR passed away, and Helen was once more at Christmas time. She has made an effort during the year. As the winter spent itself, when she reached March, and found that things were just the same— George still wrapped in his work, and still waiting, as far as she was concerned—Helen had wondered why she too had dropped the work. Why not go on? That would, at any rate, put an end to her idleness. And workers were needed. At first she had no idea of going on alone; not for a moment did the thought cross her mind. But now she moved. Moreover, she felt that she was losing all her friends, and she took no fancy to any of the people with whom George was becoming acquainted.

This resolve brought with it a painful feeling. She felt sure that when George saw her going to work again, he would be greatly relieved. The more she brooded over this, the more bitter the thought became until at last it grew into an agony such as she had never known. She would not then be on his conscience, because he could always think that she was occupied and interested, and he would be freer. She was not even sure whether a dim feeling of this kind was not partly the reason that her idleness oppressed her; perhaps it was partly because she hated to see him uneasy that she began to work again.

She went once more to meetings, and renewed her friendship with the old set of people. She even tried writing some articles. But it was miserable. There seemed to be no reason for what she did. Nobody wanted her. She even went hopelessly back to some of the social work which they had discarded at the beginning, for there seemed more need of her there. But she was not doing it for any one's sake, and there was no longer a feeling of strength and certainty in the work.

George had gone on contributing to the paper. Sometimes he wrote character sketches; sometimes he wrote descriptions of places which had struck him, containing perhaps the faintest tinge of human interest—a craftsman at work in his shop window, dignified; a nurse-maid wheeling her perambulator up and down the one piece of smooth pavement in a new outskirt of Berlin, with the peculiar swagger in the swinging motion of the body, pleased that a man in a balcony should be watching her—just such a tiny thread by which he meant the description to hold together.

But often a week or two would pass without any contribution to the paper, when he thought that he saw his way to a proper expression of some bit of the great Wilmersdorf novel. This work often gave him trouble, and sometimes brought him to desperation. But it was his business, and he never felt hopeless for long; he would know how to do it soon. However, when the summer came, the novel was still chaotic; the sketch was complete, but very little of it was really finished. He had arranged to stay in London during August, Bishop went to Dieppe for a holiday with his family. In September Henry came back, and George and Helen went to Dieppe, where the Bishops were still staying. George was in the middle of a period of the most warm affection for the whole Bishop family. Helen found the mother and father dull, even a little common; Henrietta she disliked.

Heinrich Bishop, the father of Henry and Henrietta, was a German from Hamburg, where his father, an Englishman, had settled in his boyhood. Heinrich had married a little German girl, and remained in his father's business until a few years after the birth of Henrietta, when he came to London to take charge of a new branch of the business, and settled near Westbourne Park. In England he became ultra-English. The English pose was a continual vexation to his wife, who was a regular housewife, and a source of much amusement to his father, really an Englishman, and quite contented to live in Hamburg. In fact, the father's sarcasms about his son's Anglomania annoyed the son more than he confessed. Henrietta, who was a great favourite of her father's, never could agree with her mother. Since they had very few friends, she was always pining to go to the subscription dances, races, regattas, cricket matches, skating rinks—anywhere to be among people; and as her mother hated receiving or going out, and would have liked Henry to help her in the house, vaguely wishing she would employ her time with heaven knows what serious occupation, the girl had to depend for her pleasures a good deal upon chance acquaintances; and this was another source of annoyance to her mother. Mr. Bishop would reply, when his wife complained, that the remedy lay in her own hands; and as for being idle, English women as a rule did not spend much time in housekeeping.

Heinrich was proud of his English son, and had always been very lenient to him, and Henry was adored by his mother. He had at first been sent to University College School. Next it was decided that he should go to Sandhurst. For that purpose he went to a crammer's for a year. When he looked back upon that year, it seemed to resolve itself into one long, hot summer day of boredom in class, a walk down the Grove with some other men in straw hats, and an evening of empty fooling in the Gardens where they lived. After he had spent the year at the crammer's he gave up the army, thinking that he was fit for something better. It was just at the period when he tool to Shelley and began to talk about Balzac. He would go to Cambridge and try for the Bar. Mrs. Bishop had objected to the Sandhurst scheme, and had hated the life her son led at the crammer's. Cambridge was not so bad; but really she would have liked him to go into his father's business. The boy himself did not know what he wished to do; but he felt enthusiastic and advanced, and enthusiastic and advanced he entered at Trinity.

Helen disliked Henrietta, disliked everything about her; the rather forward manner, a bold outside covering a nature really timid from shallowness and incapable of taking a strong line and of actually facing any difficulty, and this joined with a perpetual and obvious desire to be in society and to be seem, which led her continually into open differences with her mother, and which seemed to be the whole life of the girl. So far there was a good deal of truth in Helen's observation. But she was unfair when she put down what seemed to her a preposterous admiration for George's work to affectation and a general wish to flatter any man in order to attach him. Henrietta really believed that George was very clever, and she was flattered by the attention which he paid her. If she imagined that her admiration was more for his art than it really was, that was not affection, but a mistake.

George was flattered at the admiration, and felt that she was flattered merely by his giving her his company, and as she showed very plainly her great wish for society and enjoyment, he felt inclined to do all he could to supply her need. It had always been a pleasure to him to take any amount of trouble for people who at all pleased him, if he felt that they needed him enough to be touched by his attentions.

George began a great work in Dieppe. One afternoon he happened to leave the Casino and the region of hotels and gaiety, and in the course of a walk through the town he came upon the docks and basins which had been lately been built at great expense. There were hardly any ships in them, the enormous warehouses were empty, and had the peculiarly desolate look of things which have never been used, the railway lines were rusty, the arms of the cranes pointed meaninglessly into the sky. Everything had been done on the lavish scale. He came back with the idea of the town a failure, dead at the core, and only living at the edge, just along the plage where the visitors came in the summer.

He was greatly excited at this idea. Gradually it took shape as the life of the town, the real life which goes in all the year, contrasted with the gay passing life of visitors during the season, the centre of the picture. He fired Henrietta's admiration afresh when he told her of this: really it did look magnificent.

Helen had paid no attention to George's stories in themselves; it has not struck her to look at them critically for a moment. But now that she felt thar the solitary effort to continue the social work was no comfort, now that she was entirely cut off from it and idle in Dieppe, and heard Henrietta in raptures over her husband's writing, she unconsciously took to reading his sketches carefully. It was only when she had already criticised two or three, that she realised that this was the first time she had really looked at her husband's new work, although he had been writing for ten months. It had never entered into her head that the question whether his stories were good or bad might be of any importance to her. The gradual discovery that he had really gone back from his proper work to this had been enough to occupied her thoughts.

And her criticism was adverse. Naturally she came biassed to the consideration; but still, truly enough, she could see nothing in the sketches. They were either shapeless and utterly incomprehensible, or else they were so slight as to be nothing at all. She read the three articles containing the sketch of Wilmersdorf, and she remembered bits of what she had heard from himself and others of his long novel on the subject. That would be another shapeless production, more shapeless than ever. And when, in his joy at the discovery of this new Dieppe picture, he told her something about it, that was just the same. And what was this idea of always writing about towns? Who ever heard if taking such a thing as a town for the subject of a novel, as if it were a person? And when next he spoke to her of it, she said that this business of towns was becoming a mania with him, and no one would understand what he meant.

They went back to London at the beginning of October. Helen began again with her work, but with less hope than ever. And gradually she dropped her friends, and left off working bit by bit, though it was Christmas before she had quite stopped. One of her regular occupations had been to attend a certain committee-meeting on Wednesday evenings, and that was one of the last things to which she held.

But one Wednesday evening soon after Christmas she had not the heart to go. She was sitting, spiritless and tired, in the drawing-room. George always went to dine at the Bishops' on Wednesday evenings. He came in at eleven o'clock in good spirits. He had noticed already that Helen had been leaving off work gradually, and when he found her in the drawing-room, looking as if she had been at home all the evening, he asked at once—

"Haven't you been to your meeting?" "No."

"Oh! So you dropped off the work, too, then?"

Helen looked at him, astonished; then she stretched out both her arms over her chair, not towards him, but despairingly, anywhere, her head bowed forward upon them; great sobs suddenly broke from her, hopeless sobs. And crying still, she rocked herself to and fro. She let George come and kneel by her side and take her hand and speak softly to her; but that was no comfort. What he had said seemed to her so hideously cruel: he had sneered, simply because she shoved how utterly her life depended upon him, after her humble attempt to work on alone—thinking of him even then. George did not understand. He had not meant anything particular by remark. Even as he kissed her forehead and her brown hair and tried to comfort her, he knew that he was out of sympathy with her. As he knelt by her side he was thinking all the time that her sorrow could not last. How was it possible when his work was so wonderful and he felt so hopeful in it? His confidence was so strong, it must conquer everything; so he fixed his eyes obstinately at a point beyond her present pain.

That night Helen wondered how she would be able to go on living. Something must happen to make her sorrow less vast and high, to break it into smaller pieces and bring it down to earth, making it more like what were called troubles. She could not live at this stretch.

XIV.

IN January a collection of George's sketches came out. A publisher who had a great idea that it was useful to appear advanced and strange, offered to bring them out if George would share in the expense.

Helen had imagined that there would be an outcry when George's change of face became known. A man who had devoted himself so entirely to social work, and who had made a name for himself by taking a distinct line which every one respected, could not change round just at the moment of success without notice. But no, there had been no outcry. No one seemed to think it astonishing that a socialist should take to writing stories. Some of the critics even, in writing of the volume, spoke as if they saw no break in his work. He had published some extreme essays; now here were some absurd stories.

Most of the papers made great fun of the book. As soon as Bishop's paper became at all known, it had afforded endless chaff and laughter week after week, so that when the stories reappeared, the critics were on the alert, and they simply rollicked. One especially, a rising man, wrote a most happy article upon the book; he had never been so inspired. There was something really grand, he said, about the childlike simplicity with which Mr. Aston seriously wrote and offered to the public such amazingly idiotic things—no, not idiotic, for that was unpleasant, but baby-like. The critic reveled in the solemn fatuousness of Mr. Aston, and his article had a great success. The literary people asked each other whether they had seen Monty Frere's article about Aston's book, and then they chuckled and roared over every line of it.

Frere was delighted with the success of his article, because his idea was to make himself famous as a literary critic. There were men who had become known in a short time by their dramatic and art criticisms; not he would make a name in this way.

The publisher was not disappointed, for the book was much talked of. People bought it in order to join in the laugh. The way in which his book was treated reminded George of a short stay which he had made in an out-of-the-way French village a long time ago. The inhabitants remarked upon his clothes, and his fame spread, until at last the tiny children, who would never have noticed anything strange about him, and had no idea of what their elders were laughing at, used to run out when he passed, and collect round him when he stopped, and stand gazing at one another for a minute or two, until one of them would giggle, and then they all roared with laughter and ran away.

George knew that there were faults in the stories, but he was sure that they were not so ridiculous as the critics made out. He did not pay very much attention to what they said; sometimes it made him a little sad; but the immoderate fun and laughter, the extreme self-satisfaction and positiveness of some, roused in him a spirit of fight. He settled down with energy to "Wilmersdorf" once more, for the Dieppe novel he could not finish, though he had brought it to the same point as the other.

Helen happened to mention Frere's article in the course of the conversation—

"Oh, but I know Frere. He's one of those horrible sneaking little men, a kind of rat, whom no man would speak to if he followed his private opinion. Besides, no one could possibly take his article for criticism; you can see with half an eye that he has stolen a couple of points from some one or other, and then has been inspired with this funny article; it certainly is funny. He hasn't a scrap of insight; he's sure to succeed in making himself the crack literary critic, which is what he wants to do."

George made merry over the criticism, and at heart, too, he often felt that it was amusing to be one man against every one's derision. But his wife could not feel like that. It was terrible. She was ashamed to go out for fear of seeing a friend. She had not paid attention to what the world had said of the paper; but now she was brought with a shock right up against her husband's work and its worth. And that George should go gaily on to more ridicule after this disgrace, brush criticism aside, and say that it meant nothing—her face burned to think of it. And there was no possible feeling of martyrdom; he was fighting for no cause. It was indeed fatuous, as they said.

Margaret came to see her, and Helen was fearful lest something should lead to the dreaded subject. After a few minutes' conversation Margaret said—

"I think George's stories read charmingly; better than when they appeared in the paper."

Helen thought that she was only saying that to comfort her. It was not like Margaret to do such a thing, for she was too sensitive to comfort in that way; but they had seen so little of each other during the most important part of Helen's life that the were almost strangers. But she thought that it was too cruel when, after a murmured "Yes?" Margaret went on—

"Don't you think so?"

Helen bit her lip, but it was no use—she was crying. She got up from her chair and walked to the window—just such a girlish movement as Margaret had often seen her make. As the instant Margaret was back again in their old loving school-days. She went up to her and put her arms around her.

"But, Helen, my sweet Helen, you don't really mind what they say?"

Helen could not answer for her crying, indeed she had no answer to that question, for her tears came from further away.

"They are all mistaken. They will change their mind. I'm not so enthusiastic, am I, that I'm likely to go off my head suddenly? When I read the first story in the paper it did strike me as strange; but then I went back and like the first. It's only a question of knowing them. Anybody with sense, who has once got over the obvious strangeness, couldn't help seeing how honest and truthful all his things are. And as for the strangeness, which they make so much of, it would need a clever man to say for certain that even that mayn't be the beginning of something new which we shall all admire in a few years."

Helen hardly listened to what Margaret was saying, but she was grateful. Margaret's heart smote her when she saw Helen like this. Why had she neglected her friend, and taken it for granted that everything was right with her? And this regret showed itself in Margaret's comforting love, and Helen, too, felt that they were as close as they used to be.

And gradually Margaret learnt the whole truth, which Helen had vaguely imagined she knew somehow—and Margaret had not even known that she did not admire George's work.

This long explanation with Margaret was a great comfort to Helen. And yet, as she thought over it that night, with a great shock there suddenly came into her mind the indignation she would have shown when she was a girl if she had been told that she could ever confide in any one, any one however dear, about her married life—and now it was a relief!

Still, for all that she was shocked, she felt much stronger when, facing George, she could remember that Margaret knew her whole sorrow. She did not feel so weighed down, as with a sense of utter defeat.

All through February Aston was struggling with "Wilmers-dorf." He was in great difficulties, and often he would spend whole days doing nothing. Helen could not understand the days of idleness. If he was going to do this work, why did he not at least do it? George, meanwhile, in great need of sympathy, wanting some one to whom he could talk until he grew confident in his theories, began to confide in Helen.

He was telling the story of "Wilmersdorf" by means of the history of two or three families; and the whole thing was written rather from the standpoint of the innkeeper's daughter, who is left as waitress when her father is bought out. Now George's difficulty was to keep the book to its real point—the expression of a change in a village—and yet not to give himself away by crudely stating the case. He told Helen that he had decided not to write any more character-sketches for the paper. He had come to the conclusion that they were thoroughly bad, for they increased his natural tendency to be explanatory. None of the fools who had criticised his story had said that; and it was the one thing to say. He seemed to Helen to be quite as much pleased with the discovery that his stories were bad as he could have been if he had found out that they were perfect. He would correct his fault by taking up some of his work and re-writing it in play form; there was no possibility of explanation in the dialogue of a play.

Helen could not imagine that any work could be done in that way. And she was astonished that he could go one against such discouragement, though his perseverance seemed less to be respected than to be pitied. And then his great and only objection to his stories was not the real objection at all.

In the course of his work George made a discovery which interested him, and he could not contain his delight when he came to tell Helen.

"I haven't been able to get through much work actually the last two days; but in thinking how things should be done I've found out something. It's absurd to suppose that a man is always executing; he must spend a lot of time without doing anything, thinking out his difficulties."

He had discovered the reason why Ibsen introduces symbols into his plays; for he himself had felt the need for a symbol of some kind in the course of his own work. In his novel about Wilmersdorf his tendency had been to keep more and more to the history of the girl, and leave out the change in the village, which was the real reason for the story's existence. That he might keep the gradual change always in view, without stating over and over again the facts of the case—as Zola often did—he had found himself thinking of some actual object—a mound in the inn-garden, a piece of furniture, or a corner house, or perhaps such a thing as an old village custom—which suffers by the change, and so is a continual expression of it. In fact, a symbol which would stand for the great idea in the book, and do away with explanations and restatements—a perpetual metaphor.

"As we are realists, of course the symbol isn't extravagant, but takes a place in the scene, only having a special significance all the time parallel to the story."

At first the village was orderly, because it was peaceful and unknown; then it became disorderly, because of the change, and finally it ended by being orderly once more, when the irresistible force of the town had come and fashioned it to its uses. He had felt of his own accord the necessity for a symbol, and then suddenly had come into his head the wooden bridge over the mill-stream in "Rosmersholme," the crack in the chimney, the high tower in the "Master Builder."

And was not that exactly the reason for which Ibsen had put in these things? Without the symbols those plays would either have been incomplete and incomprehensible, or else Ibsen would have been forced to stuff them full of explanations.

He became so excited over his discovery that in talking to Helen his voice towards the end unconsciously sounded with the eager intonation of the actress who had interpreted those plays. Helen could not understand why George should make such a fuss about all this and talk about it; and she was still more annoyed when a fortnight afterwards he said—

"Of course no one can use the symbol after Ibsen. It's all right with him, and it's beautiful; but it must be really a mistake in expression, and it would be mannered and sill in others. Still, it's useful to see how people get round their difficulties."

Helen could not see her way through all these theories; they seemed to have no use, and she distrusted them. And then, for some reason which she could not at all understand, whenever he talked as he had done about his discovery, her moral sense was shocked. He said nothing indecent or blasphemous, and yet she was hurt and made miserable. And she felt the same when she read any bits which he had finished and gave her to see, until at last she thought she could not read any more.

Margaret came often to see her, and was a great comfort. Helen said—

"I can't at all see things as he does, and though I understand what he actually says, this theorising seems so useless. And he's perfectly contented. It's growing at last to be a tyranny, for his theories are all I get from him, and he talks of them in a selfish way to please himself. And quite unimportant things, such as the best hours for work, or explanations why he does not work…. The whole thing is torture to me. I'm sure there are people who could shrug their shoulders or even be amused; but I can't possibly. It oppresses me. I wish I could get to feel more like an outsider sometimes—I always feel so terribly concerned."

Margaret did not know how to console her; but she spoke lovingly to her and said that she must wait.

"And it's all the worse coming after those first three years. I suppose most women haven't had such a complete union as that, and so they can go on one way and let their husbands go another more easily—perhaps they don't need it."

"But George hasn't changed, as far as I can see."

"Changed so much that life isn't recognisable."

"Still, though he may think and talk of different things now, he's there himself."

"Neither of us seems to be able to make that distinction—at least I can't. I daresay he could, for any one seems now to be able to get more of him than I can."

By the end of July George had finished "Wilmersdorf." There were pieces of it which he left in an unsatisfactory state, and here and there he had broken his own principles. But he was sure he had given due prominence to the original idea, and had not sacrificed it to the story. The same publisher promised to bring it out in October. George began to write for the paper again. He had forsaken it for some time, and had also seen less of the set, except Harry, who was always with him, for he had fancied that he could work better if he was more alone. His reappearance was hailed with delight. The set had changed a little. Those who found that they were writing nearer the public taste than the rest of the staff, deserted their first friends—some prefixing a quarrel to their desertion; others sending less and less important work as success gradually claimed them.

XV.

DURING the latter half of August Helen and George went to Dieppe and took Margaret with them. It was Helen's idea to take her; she needed her companionship, and Margaret and George liked each other. Helen admired the way in which she would banter George about his theories; but then she remembered that his ways were not Margaret's concern, and that neither of them made any demands upon the other, so that her freedom was not so wonderful.

At the beginning of September Margaret left them to join Mrs. Forde; and Henry Bishop, who had been at Dieppe with his family, went back to London to take over the paper for which he and George had been writing during the month.

Helen missed Margaret painfully. Since her departure it had grown cold and rainy, and the second week of September began with a great storm.

The next week it was worse still; people said that there had been no such storm for ten years. In the afternoon George and Henrietta Bishop had gone off to look at the sea from the pier, and Mr. and Mrs. Bishop, finding Helen sitting alone and reading a book in a corner of the Casino gallery, brought their chairs up and talked to her. Both Mr. and Mrs. Bishop were fond of George, Mrs. Bishop especially had a weakness for him; and they were both a little afraid of Helen, Mrs. Bishop more than her husband; for beside being a clever, advanced woman, and the wife of the great George, she seemed to her to have such superiority over other wives. She was so thoroughly at one with her husband, that she had none of the ordinary weaknesses of women; for instance, she did not mind his leaving her for hours together alone at the Casino. They would hardly have dared to sit by her now, but Helen asked them to keep her company, for there was something in their simplicity which appealed strongly to her in her present state of mind.

George and Henrietta were walking briskly along the windy plage towards the pier. While they were passing through the Casino on their way out, they talked of the people who passed by them, wondering how the members of a particular party were related, or fixing on distinguished looking old men the names of celebrated people who were said to be at Dieppe. On the plage it was so noisy and boisterous that they talked very little, only now and then calling each other's attention to the waves which were breaking over the lighthouse.

When they reached the harbor, they joined a group of townspeople and visitors who were standing on the hinder part of the pier, watching the waves, and discussing whether there was any danger that part of the masonry might give way. No one expected the boat to start from Newhaven in such weather; but some time before three o'clock, an old sailor with a telescope cried out that he saw it. Every one strained their eyes; there was much pointing and much blindness; but at last the whole group had seen the speck, and settled itself down to the enjoyment of watching the gradual approach of the steamer. Some Englishmen among the party argued about the distance of the boat from the pier, and as this British habit was a common joke with the set, George and Henrietta looked at each other and laughed. The speck grew larger and larger, and at last the steamer was sweeping and heaving its way in between the two piers.

A great number of people had gathered at the landing-place to see the boat arrive. George and Henrietta hurried back from the pier and joined the crowd. The boat had just come to a standstill, and everybody was peering down at the deck. Suddenly a cloud came over the faces of the townspeople who were standing by, and George heard them mutter and point to the boat. He turned his face from them and looked once more upon the deck. There he saw a man, deadly pale, with his legs bandaged lying upon a stretcher. As the hooks of the crane were being fixed into the stretcher the murmurs of the crowd grew louder. The chain moved and the people began to hiss. The man was swung up from the boat and over the heads of the spectators, who were by that time hissing loud, groaning and shouting out curses. Henrietta felt afraid, and took hold of George's hand—the piteous sight of the crowd, and all so sudden and unexpected and mysterious. The man was let down upon a large barrow and wheeled away, while the townspeople lined up all along his path and cursed and spat and shook their fists in his face.

George and Henrietta turned homewards, without speaking; but as he passed by a woman and a man standing at the door of their shop, George asked what the man had done, and he gathered scraps of a tragic story thrown in between curses. The man was the proprietor of a café under the arcades. He had made the common people loathe him by his extraordinary cruelty and villainy. A fortnight before he had left by boat on a visit to England. The day after, when the boat returned, some people heard from the crew that on his way across he had fallen into the hold and had broken both his legs. He had evidently stayed at Newhaven Hospital, and had been sent back as soon as he could be moved; and he had come, unexpected, like a curse again upon the town, on the day of this black storm, such as had not been for years.

Henrietta and George talked little while they were walking along the Quay; but when they came into the bright, friendly Grande Rue, they spoke eagerly about what they had just seen.

"There was something so shocking about it, I felt afraid," Henrietta said.

"A minute before we noticed the man you made some laughing remark about the ball to-night."

"Yes, I remember."

"And immediately afterwards, we visitors had forced upon us a scene in a tragedy which belonged to the townspeople alone."

"The look of the crowd frightened me; they were so fierce."

"It's always a shock to be let into the life of a town which seems to us to exist only for the summer months."

"That's just the idea of your novel, isn't it?" "Yes, and the story would come in well; don't you think so? The chief theme the town and visitors, the harbour and docks a failure, and this story a lurid thread in the personal side of the book."

They talked on for some time.

"And what will the critics say of 'Wilmersdorf'?"

"They are sure, at any rate, not to find fault with the right parts. I could tell them what's wrong with myself in many places."

George liked being with Henrietta, especially in Dieppe; not because there was anything in her (though he was never ungrateful enough to say that); but because she wanted something of him, and pleased him by showing the want. And she did not want much, not more than he could give with pleasure. And there is a peculiar and lasting charm about the sister of a college friend; and Henry had always admired him, and had been the first to cheer him on. Sometimes she was really interested when he talked about his work; at other times she felt vain that he should confide in her—and sometimes she took his talk as the natural price to pa for his company. It was a most complete pleasure for her to dance with him, and that was why he enjoyed dancing with her. For besides the dancing of a good partner, she liked to be seen with one often, especially as there was a dearth of men at the Casino. She knew that Margaret did not like her, and thought her common, so that in Margaret's company she always behaved less well than usual, from a mixed feeling of uneasiness and resentment. George saw this perfectly, and used to have arguments about her with Margaret and Helen together.

When they reached the house where the Bishops were staying, George and Henrietta looked in through the open window, and surprised Mr. and Mrs. Bishop at tea. Henrietta went in and joined them; but George said he must go home, and remained outside, chatting with Mrs. Bishop for a minute. As he went away, Henrietta cried out to him not to be late at the ball that evening. Some people whom she just knew by sight had arrived from London a day or two before, and she wished to dance every dance and feel thoroughly in it, as they would certainly be at the Casino in the evening looking on.

George began thinking again of what they had seen that afternoon. It had been strangely striking, and a magnificent example of his great Dieppe idea. It really seemed as if the story would come in beautifully. At any rate, the incident set him thinking with fresh enthusiasm.

He entered the house and found Helen writing a letter. She had spent a weary afternoon, and as George came in, his customary ignoring of her real feelings pained her more than usual, for in the course of writing to Margaret she had brought her weariness to a head, and as he began to talk she felt almost bitter. After a few words, he mentioned something about her wishing to go back to London.

"How did you hear that?"

"Mrs. Bishop said that she had been so pleased to spend an hour or two with you, and in talking about leaving, she told me you'd said you'd like to go—I didn't know before."

"Yes, during a rather dull two hours with the Bishops I said so—though it was chiefly to make conversation."

"Do you really want to go?"

"Yes, I do." And as he seemed to wait for her to give an explanation, she went straight on, "I shall feel less lonely in London. Here among all these strangers it wearies me to be left alone."

George was shocked; her words were a sudden light showing up his conduct. He came and sat by her, and began—

"Oh, Helen, my own Helen, I'm so sorry; it has been horrible of me to be so careless—I didn't think—"

She had looked him in the face as he came near to her; but his grief was so obvious what she broke down, and between her sobs she said passionately—

"Oh, to be left alone, always, always alone! And here in the Casino! And the people sit and wonder why I'm always alone, and I willingly accept the pity of people like the Bishops. Oh, it's unbearable! And often when I'm alone there, I see you with other people, and you never come and speak to me, not even as an acquaintance would!" And her cry was broken by the passion of her tears.

"But Helen, Helen, it's not like that! I didn't think at the moment; everything went on so easily. I didn't hurt you purposely!"

And as he appealed to her, bitterly repenting of his thoughtlessness during the long month which could never be recalled, her tears gained him, and he could speak no more, and say crying too.

And when she cried no longer he was still sobbing heavily, with his face between his hands. And every sorrow of which he had ever dreamt came to mingle with his anguish at having so hurt his wife.

Helen was tired out with crying, and turned to him, for she could not bear to see him still racked with sobs. She had never seen him cry before. And she comforted him, and stroked his hair, and said she was sorry, that she had not meant to say anything during this holiday, but had hoped they would go back quietly to London soon.

For a long time she could not comfort him, nor even stay his sobbing, for George did not know himself how his grief came to be so complex.

The servant came in to lay cloth, and George left his chair, and went to the window. When they had finished dinner Helen said—

"You will go to the Casino to-night?" "No, I don't think I'll go."

"But why not? Oh, please go."

"I couldn't enjoy myself; that's the only reason."

"But, poor Henrietta, it will disappoint her so!"

"Yes, I'm sorry to disappoint her, and it's no fault of hers." Indeed he was sorry; it seemed so shamefully unkind—in fact, part of his whole grief was because the pleasant, easy friendship between them seemed to have been all a mistake.

"But it puts me in such a false position; as if I could wish to stop any pleasure of yours!"

"You're not stopping it—it's my own fault if I can't go. And then I should like to be with you this evening, it's the only way I could pass it with any comfort."

"I promised the old lad next door to go and sit with her, and I'm afraid you can't come too; I arranged it all beforehand. I didn't wish you to feel that I depended on you, so I thought I would engage myself to-night, as I didn't want to go to the Casino...."

Helen was afraid as soon as she had said this that she had pained George again; she told him that for her sake he must not grieve so.

That night in bed Helen thought over what had happened. She had not meant to speak—and then when she had spoken there had come this cry of being left alone for the company of others. But that was not the real grievance, she knew that well enough; and yet she had naturally complained of this neglect, this had come into her mind painfully, the complaint of any or- dinary woman. It did not seem to her like her own self, like her old character, to stop at the outside without going to the truth.

They stayed two more days in Dieppe, and both were pleased to be always together. Yet George's pleasure was dashed with a sentimental regret at the thought of leaving a place which he loved so much, under this shadow which had been thrown back upon the visit; and he was sorry for Henrietta, and even the dark story which they had come upon added to his melancholy; and vaguely the thought of his work troubled him. So that through his pleasure at sitting by Helen's side there ran a regret, a yearning which made him soft, weak like a man after a fever.

And Helen knew, if only from his not working, that he was not in his normal state, and went on half considering how things really stood, and half simply contented that they were together.

XVI.

IN October "Wilmersdorf" appeared. George had finished the proofs in Dieppe, and Henrietta had been pleased to help him: he saw that Helen hated the book, and would rather not look at it. The change of face on the publication of "Wilmersdorf" was interesting. Monty Frere became moral, and the mass of critics followed faithfully and raised up their hands. They none of them explained what they meant. It was not exactly the story of the innkeeper's daughter which shocked them, though perhaps something in the perfectly even treatment of her story may have had a share in hurting their moral sense. The author took her ruin for granted, and treated it as if he himself had no moral feelings at all—which was the fact, for he had been entirely taken up with another aspect of the circumstances. And the more simple, taking it for granted that the final stage of the village was meant to be happy, especially as the author called it "Order," were fearfully shocked by his diabolical want of the ordinary moral attributes of mankind. Fancy leading his heroine and her village up to orderly vice, vice without question, as the summit of ambition! It was unheard of! They had articles about the state regulation of prostitution, with letters from "English women," they went far afield and filled many pages of their papers with print which people eagerly read.

At first Aston stood aghast at their stupidity, and at the apparently unquenchable fire he had innocently kindled: he even thought of pointing out how they had gone wrong. But as they went on further and further, the humour of the thing struck him suddenly, and he shouted, shouted with laughter for a whole day. If he stopped laughing a moment, a new side of the affair, more ridiculous than the others set him off in a fresh fit.

George saw to some extent what even the less simple people found shocking. He had been at great pains to show that in the intermediate stage the villagers ruined themselves by trying to do something for which they were not fitted. Whether it was the innocent attempt to supply the visitors with beer, or the less innocent attempt to make successful love to the men, was all the same for his purpose. And his own perfect innocence in conscientiously working out his idea without ever dreaming of morality, added humour to the affair of the critics.

But he found that Helen felt with them, as she had done before. Indeed, when he laughed she could not help showing him that she was sure they were right. She had come down from her original high position, the sorrow at his having left the work, and the hope that he would return: and now she found herself begging him to write something less horrible and disgusting. It was no use assuring her that it was impossible there could be anything immoral in the book: it was only a certain treatment which came naturally to him, and was new to them. People were always inclined to think that a new handling in any art is indecent.

But in contradiction to the universal howl, the book gained for Aston the beginning of a following. If any one outside his own personal admirers had liked his volume of stories, George had not heard of it. But on the appearance of "Wilmersdorf," three or four critics sided with him, and behind them he felt the force of a certain number of admirers, a force that felt as if it would grow. Quite a large section of these admirers were enthusiastic. Whatever faults the book had, it was an endeavour far above the level of contemporary English novels, and Aston would do great things. The chief critic who praised his book was a man who had formerly done some work for the paper. He admired George, and now although he was successful and had advanced greatly during the last year or two, his admiration remained. A well-established and well-known weekly had taken work of his regularly, though his exceedingly modern articles showed somewhat strangely in the rest of the paper. Thus Aston had strong praise from a most important quarter. And George received another piece of praise, which flattered him still more. It came from a famous novelist, for whom he had always had a certain admiration, which was now greatly increased. He was an old man by this time, nearly sixty. His reputation had come slowly and gently. There had never been any great excitement about his work, either for or against it; he had never advertised himself and had never been boomed; but gradually his books had taken a higher and higher place in public opinion. He could never have been popular; but probably at this time the majority of people who had claims to taste would have put him first among English contemporary writers.

He liked Aston's book, and as he knew Miss Spencer and Mrs. Lemardelay, it was not difficult to bring about a meeting. He asked him to his house, and took a fancy to him. He had a step-daughter, a woman between thirty and forty. She had written some fine stories; but after her mother's death she had devoted herself entirely to her step-father, whom she adored, and had written very little. George naturally fell in love with this woman, a talented writer herself, and the favourite of the great man for whom she lived, and in whose genius she seemed to have a share. George did not see much of her; but the names of the lady and the step-father were always on his lips, he raved about them.

Helen went once or twice with him to see them. She admired the man himself; but his liking for George had no effect upon her. It was not to the point. He knew nothing about their life, and how things had happened, and if he had discovered that George was a clever man, which all the world knew, what was that to her? It was simply another thing for George to rave about. She knew the step- daughter slightly, and her devotion was certainly beautiful; but it irritated Helen to hear George, who had so little power of devotion, always praising her for that. Besides, she had admired and even known the genius years and years ago, and why should he suddenly be extolled as if no one had ever heard of him before?

During the two years which had passed, when George thought of Helen, he had refused to consider her sorrow as if it were a fixed reality. His work was so wonderful that he persisted in ignoring her thoughts. And then he had come to believe that he would soon reach a position of security, a height from which he could safely look and consider things—they must both wait until that time. And he had waited and hoped that she would wait, working hard in his own way, not having the heart to face the difficulty at the beginning before he felt secure himself.

But he never seemed to arrive at that point. And now, after two years, when he felt how utterly out of sympathy she was with his work and with all his ways, he began to justify himself to his own mind. And this change appeared when he talked to Helen.

"George, the Maxwells are always asking after you, and wondering why you never go to see them."

"They get on my nerves rather, those people. Their minds are so completely moral and social. I really have no point of contact with them."

The Maxwells were a married couple with whom the Astons had been very friendly in the first three years of their marriage, and Helen was still fond of them; they were almost the last friends of that period with whom she had kept up an acquaintance.

"But you used to like them so much."

"Oh, no, not really. I've nothing against them, I simply can't get on with them. They are just the same as all the ridiculous people who've been talking morality over my book instead of criticising it, their state of mind is incomprehensible to me, that's all."

"It was only a few years ago that you were working side by side with them."

"I should hardly call that 'working side by side': I was finding out that what they cared about was rubbish. That's all I ever did during those three years. And when I reached the one thing which was not rubbish—I had had enough."

"Then your socialism meant nothing?"

But without waiting for an answer she hurried on to another subject and then went away.

George only saw that he was vindicating himself. His art and his own feelings had so completely engrossed him that he could not have understood what Helen felt as she listened to his scraps of justification. Helen only saw that he was incredibly cruel and cowardly in belittling the work which they had discovered, and trying to exonerate himself from the responsibility even of having joined in it. And she who had longed so for sympathy and an occupation, and had found so perfect a satisfaction, was now alone and without any occupation except to brood over his sneers at her discovery.

And there was something which was always urging her on to hear more from him.

"The idea of my imagining that I was that sort of person, a 'Sozial-Kopf'! Why, I set about objecting and criticising at once, and with great delight. All my opinions are in those articles— and almost all are hostile! Even my objections were not the objections of a moral and social person, but rather of an artist."

And when she asked him why he had ever taken to socialism, he said—

"Oh, I was an enthusiastic young fool with 'Welt-Schmerz.'"

She was maddened. Their divine gospel, and her exquisite influence, and her George as she had loved him, everything, everything was to be recklessly smirched in order to leave nothing but his art and his theories. And his unconsciousness, which kept her from raving at him when he grew too cruel, completed her misery.

"There's all the difference in the world. What I did before wasn't work—I was occupied, that was all. Now I've got beyond that. I've found real work, my work, the affair of my life. It was like that humble craftsman I wrote about, seen in the window of his shop, looking seriously at the crucifix which he was finishing, with just the expression that the greatest artist has when he considers what he has done—the type of the man dignified by his work."

He did indeed seem to Helen to be possessed not to see the satire of his words. To leave his work in the cause of humanity, to entrench himself in this folly—doubly foolish, for all the world saw that he was incapable—and then to talk of the dignity of work! And all that Helen could do was to combat stray bits of his justification, illogically, hopelessly, or to run away when her pain and her scorn grew too fierce.

XVII.

HENRY had for some time been tiring of the paper. He had often spoken about it to George, and at last, in March, they decided the paper should stop. George had no great wish to carry it on, though he was pleased to write for it when he chose, and no one else appeared to take Henry's place. Towards the end of the evening when, after a meeting of the staff in Henry's chambers, they had finally decided that the next number should be the last, George and Henry were left alone. George and Henry were left alone. George was talking about his "Dieppe," for he was in difficulties as usual over the book.

"It's quite true that in 'Wilmersdorf' the story of the girl served its purpose well enough; and though somehow it seems a pity to weigh down a pretty thing like that with a huge, cumbrous idea, I don't see that there was any way out of it."

"No, I don't either. Certainly the change in the village was rather an oppressive weight for simple little Lieschen to carry!"

"Well, I sha'n't make that mistake in my 'Dieppe,' for I've made up my mind now not to use the story of that man."

"Oh? But I thought it would suit so perfectly?"

"No, I don't think it would be right to use it, and I'll tell you why. You see when Henry and I saw that man being carried off that afternoon the situation struck us as tragic. It was a good example of what I mean by the town life and the visitor's life. We were visitors, thinking of dancing and the Casino, and come to amuse ourselves by looking at the rough sea, when suddenly we were plumped down in the middle of a town tragedy. It was a striking example. But that's no reason for putting the history of that man into my book. Because it gave me a fresh impulse in the working out of my vision there's no need to work it in."

"No, perhaps not. It's like telling people what the actual circumstances were which gave you the idea of a novel. No, I think you're right."

"Of course I am. And, like an idiot, I've been driving along all this time on the wrong road. It's a great mistake the way people laugh at theories and principles, as if they weren't any use; if I'd only stuck to principles I should have seen the absurdity of confounding together the case I'm describing with what I happened to see."

"Well, the time hasn't been lost: one must learn the right way by going all the wrong was first, apparently."

And they talked on, evolving principles of expression.

Henry dropped the paper, and with it he ceased writing. He had grown tired of his rather scattered life in chambers and of his enthusiasms. He gave up his rooms and went back to life at home, and it seemed to him quite natural to find himself going to his father's office—not definitely, but just to see.

He had been the first to admire George's work, and to urge him on to write; and all along he was his confidant, leading him on, the facile, imitative friend encouraging the slow, struggling man of original feelings. Then suddenly he deserted him, and George was alone, like some great sailing- ship left at the mouth of the harbor on its way out on a grey afternoon, lonely, rocking heavily.

George, then, began his "Dieppe" again, leaving out the story of the restaurant-keeper. The difficulties seemed insurmountable, for what he wished to express in this case was something still less than personal than in "Wilmersdorf," still more a concern of a town and its buildings. Moreover, the limit of

"Wilmersdorf" was fixed, there was an obvious beginning and an obvious end—the whole story of the village lasted the lifetime of one individual. But this affair of the real life of Dieppe continuing right through the year contrasted with the few weeks' visit of strangers bent on enjoyment, and behind this obvious contrast, the failure of the town's great venture as a port, and the continued success of the hotels and Casino, then the actual buildings in which the fishermen and the inhabitants live, the docks and cranes which the visitors never even see, contrasted with the Casino and the plage which they never leave—that was more difficult to manage.

He hardly knew how to begin, and for days he did nothing; often he could not even keep his mind fixed on the subject, until he thought he must be ill or tired. And at the moment there was no sympathetic person to whom he could turn. Sometimes he could almost have confided in Helen again; but then he felt how utterly hostile she was: and he himself began to feel like a tyrant when she sat speechless and he dilated on his difficulties. Then he knew that she was noticing his idleness, and that she found it incomprehensible, and therefore inexcusable. No, he would have to depend on himself, and when the work was done, then perhaps she would see—when people admired it.

George's course of self-justification, and the impossibility of saying anything in answer to him in that state, coming after so many tortures, had made Helen bitter. And when she looked at herself to have had no fixed nature when she was a girl—except that she was upright and fearless, and had a longing for something clear and strong and complete. She knew that her love and her marriage had brought out all the exquisite and diviner possibilities in her, and had given her a nature strong and devoted, capable of the most wonderful efforts. But now what was she becoming? "And in this new life of George's what is my place? Nothing; nothing for me. To be no one after having been everything! Of no account, absolutely no account. It was my life, my whole being; but now when he talks of his work, it appears to have been three years mistaken, wasted." And when she came down to actualities, she found him idle day after day, incomprehensibly idle in the cause of his art, which was ridiculous or hateful.

And it was just at the time when she was saying to herself that she was of no use and might as well not exist, that something happened to make her add—without indignation, with no sense of being wronged therein; but rather in scorn of herself—"except…"

When the paper was started, the Bishops, the Astons, and one or two others had paid down a certain sum of money. This fund lasted only a short time, and no one paid any more. Now the account was to be settled, and it was when Helen paid her share that she made the scornful exception to her uselessness.

George at once saw the affair in a more everyday light: it struck him as unjust that Helen should have to pay for something which was entirely his business, and which she even hated. Until now the question of Helen's money had never entered his head, and Helen even now did not think of the money actually paid.

"I'm sorry to ask you to pay this money. But it's only a loan. Soon my work with pay for itself."

"You know it isn't the money I care about!"

George did not answer. He shut his eyes, and strengthened himself in the old determination to wait till he reached a height where he felt safe, and from which he could see clearly. Helen thought it unfeeling in him to keep to the minor question—so insignificant, indeed, as to be beside the point.

But when month after month passed away, and got nothing out of life, the idea gradually worked its way into her mind, and grew familiar there, that George was spending her money and giving her nothing in return. She hated himself for thinking so; but still there was the thought, a constant companion. She could no longer remain on the heights, she felt the universal need of coming down to things on the ground which can be handled.

George sense of the injustice had given him a new incentive to work.

"It's no good trying any other kind of writing, I must go on as I've begun. It would be simply bad policy to leave off this particular struggle with my 'Dieppe,' when I've already spent so much time over it. Everything has to be learnt, and whatever other kind of story I might take up, I should have to go through a preliminary course—it's no easier to write sensational novels than masterpieces."

So he argued. But as days went on, and success did no come at once, the sense of injustice wore off somewhat

He had not been making a fortune when he socialist; there had never been any likelihood that he would, nor was it even expected of him. He had been, as a matter of fact, living on her money then; and after all a man's work is his own affair, it is hardly possible or right for any one to come in and make stipulations about it.

Helen's anger at herself and contempt at her meanness, instead of being of any use to her, only made her more difficult. And when they were together, they were silent, or else everything which one of them said sounded unjust or dangerous to the other. Over and over again Helen said to herself that it was wrong to let herself go, to give way to her feeling of irritation, to be silent or unsympathetic when with an effort a kindly word could be spoken. But she could not help it, she seemed really to be growing weak, while her strength was contracting itself to obstinacy and a narrow feeling of being wronged.

And George, too, when he was alone, determined that next time they were together he would be patient, and if Helen was not yielding, he would try to be frank and human, and not put off the attempt with a show of bitterness and a resignation to misunderstanding. For when he was wearied and hopeless over his work, and gently said something about it, she could not help hinting or looking disparagement. Then once he was open and did speak frankly—

"Oh! Helen, you can have no idea how you torture me. I'm almost driven to despair by my work, and then you make it worse by misunderstanding it. My position towards you harasses me enough; but you make it heavier still."

"But surely you don't feel your position towards me? You surely don't care?"

Ah! What was to be done now? She had gone off to another point and required a proof of that. For a moment he was beginning to protest; but then the bald ridicule of trying to prove such a thing in words overcame him, and he went away.

XVIII.

AT the end of April he saw his way through his "Dieppe" somewhat more clearly, and as the material was perfectly familiar to him, the work was finished sooner than he had expected, at the beginning of July. It was short, shorter than "Wilmersdorf." George was pleased that it was over at last, for he felt extraordinarily tired. Helen had been growing concerned about him, he has so thin and pale.

The publisher returned the manuscript, and told Aston that it was no use bringing out the book. Although "Wilmersdorf" was talked of, and made a beginning of admiration for Aston, it had a very small sale, and he assured him that he would be able to sell perhaps a hundred copies if this were published. The general tone of his opinion was that the first joke was all right, but that one was enough.

George was astonished at the refusal. The book was certainly an advance in one way upon "Wilmersdorf." And then for a moment it seemed to him so absurd that a man's conscientious work should not be read. He looked at the manuscript again, and he felt that whatever heaviness there was about the work, it certainly did express an idea which could not be done any other way. And certainly the idea was worth expressing.

When this disappointment came upon him, Helen grew really afraid for his heath, and before going away to the country she insisted upon taking him to a doctor. The doctor said the usual things, that he was not to dream of working for at least two months, and that he was to go and get strong on the east coast; and he told Helen that her husband would need very careful attention.

Those two months at the seaside were a delight. George kept his promise gladly, and put away all thoughts of work, not even looking forward, but enjoying the present with a gaiety and ease which made him irresistibly charming. And Helen, struck with pity when she saw how his work and his difficulties had worn him out, used up her whole nature in devotion to him. It was quite easy, neither of them had to make any effort. They never thought of mentioning the dark struggle which they had left behind them. The regret which they each felt only appeared in the eagerness with which they took up the delightful task of being sweet to one another.

These were none of those high enthusiasms perfectly shared which had given the first years of marriage in Helen's eyes such a transcending glory. But she was content to have George loving and gay and entertaining, like a boy freed from restraint.

At the end of the two months Helen wanted George to go on with her to Italy instead of returning to London. She knew that it was weak, but she felt as if she would give anything to keep him as he was.

"No, I must go back to London. Surely you wouldn't keep me idle?"

"But couldn't you work just the same if we went away together?"—so much she give in.

"No, I can work best in London. It's the place where I've been most hopeful and had the finest visions, as well as the place of darkness and struggles; and indeed, both those sides of London drag me back. It's the place for work and for everything that belongs to work."

"Oh, I dread London so!" "But don't. We shall see…"

And they hardly liked to go further than that.

But Helen was right. Directly they got back to London the old life began again. He was working—the same incomprehensible, hopeless way of working, and the enthusiasm and struggle again so strong that it tyrannized over their life—exactly the same.

He had written the story of the unfortunate man whom he had seen with Henrietta Bishop fairly completely in his first draught of "Dieppe." He now set to work upon it afresh, separating it from the "Dieppe" idea. He was sure that he felt the effect of his constant labour at those colossal subjects in the ease with which he wrote this story.

He was half way through it, when he was suddenly frightened by the thought that it was all wrong. The thing had originally struck him because of a contrast—that was really all he had seen: now he was writing the thing itself, leaving out the original reason for thinking of it all. But then he thought that after all he might as well finish it; he knew almost every word right on to the end, and there was no difficulty in his way; yes, right or wrong, he would finish it.

This book the publisher agreed to bring out.

George at one time thought that he would send it to some one else. But the idea of being offended with a man who was so business-like that he persisted in looking upon George's too conscientious work as more or less of a joke, was ridiculous.

The book appeared in March. Though admiration from any quarter flattered and pleased him, he made as light of the praise which the mass of critics gave him as he had made of their blame. "The sweep," Monty Frere, who had made himself popular by so skillfully truckling to public opinion that every one thought he was leading it, had now arrived at absolute power, and was rapidly becoming a complete bully. And in a bullying article he praised George's book, and George was divided between indignation and laughter as he read. Every one came round; there was hardly a dissentient voice. All the wiseacres said that it was very fine, "If only Aston always wrote like that!"

No one found it immoral, although, as George said, the book contained a fair proportion of the more heinous crimes in the calendar.

And Helen came round with the rest. She found the book perfect.

George had no particular affection for the story, and paid the less attention to what people said, because in a new work which seemed to him magnificent.

Helen gained very little from the success of George's book. Not that she had expected any reward for once more agreeing with general opinion. She was truly glad that the book was good; but she had taken no part in its production. She had no even been present when George got the idea of the story. It was some one else who had seen the beginning and who had received the first confidence. And she had heard no more about the work until the book was published.

George had indeed, she thought, taken an easy way out of the difficulty of their life: he never was with her. It seemed to her to be now only his weakness that stood in their way. A year ago it was she who had failed to make a real effort to be gentle and sympathetic, and absolutely to put away from her the thought of being wronged. And then that thought had become definite in the question whether George had a right to give her nothing in life when he was living upon her: from that had arisen the new fear for herself, the haunting thought that ever since the return from Berlin she had been deteriorating—that she was losing all nobility of character. But now she felt stronger: it was George who had failed. He had so little strength that he would not even wait and see how easy and sweet she could be. She would have demanded nothing of him; only trying to bring back the peace and lightness of those two summer months

121

which had passed so quickly and had apparently meant so
little. All George's strength seemed to have gone into his art.
There he was inconceivably strong. But once away from his
work, he had no strength of character left.

And Helen was always alone; more alone than she had ever
been before. George was never with her except when some of
his own friends were at the house. She disliked them all. Sometimes Helen went out with him into society; but gradually she
left off even that, for she thought that he only asked her because
it was necessary. He seemed not to care whom he made his confidant or whom he admired. He had left off talking about the genius and his step-daughter—that enthusiasm had, indeed, been
little more than talk—and in July his new admiration was for a
Mrs. Castellian, whom the had met at an "At Home"—a rich
woman with pretentions—utterly uninteresting, Helen thought.
Margaret's companionship, too, was less complete than it had
been, for she now had her own all-engrossing affair.

XIX.

MRS. FORDE, who never stayed more than a few months in one place, had rented a large manor-house near Stratford, and asked a number of the Spencers, including Margaret and her aunt, to stay with her during the spring. They were there through April and May, and enjoyed it so much that they did not come back to London at all, except Margaret, who spent the last three weeks of June there with some friends and then returned to Stratford with Helen. George could not be persuaded to go with them. Perhaps he would come with Henry and his sister for the dance which they were giving on the fifteenth of July.

But when the time came, the Bishops arrived alone, and George wrote to say that he could not leave town and break into his work just then. His publisher was agreeing to publish "Dieppe" in the autumn, and altogether he had too much to occupy him.

It was six o'clock on the morning of the sixteenth. Margaret and Henry were still in the ball-room talking. The dance had begun late, and the sunlight had fallen through the windows upon a room full of dancers. Margaret, indeed, had arranged a late dance on purpose that the dawn might find them still dancing. She had settled that one of her pleasures should be to draw aside the curtain hanging over the open window to let the daylight in upon the burning candles and the evening dresses. She remembered how at some dances in London a few of the guests had danced on till late in the morning, and then had stayed to breakfast instead of going home. She remembered the feeling of pleasant fatigue, the fresh morning air, and the look of men in dress clothes sitting down to breakfast.

The recollection was so delightful that she had set her heart on having the same pleasures on this occasion: in the country, with guests staying in the house, it would be all the easier. But people had, as a matter of fact, gone to bed before five o'clock, and only she and Henry were left. No one would have dreamed of looking after Margaret; she was a year older than Mrs. Forde, and Miss Spencer never thought of taking care of a niece who was twenty-eight.

There had been some astonishment and a good deal of vexation in Margaret Spencer's family because the girl had not married. But as far back as ten years ago Henry Bishop had paid her attentions— enough, perhaps, to make her love him; enough, at any rate, to lead her unconsciously to keep free from any attachment. Without asking the reason why, it seemed natural that she should remain free. It is true that sometimes she had imagined the possibility of his asking her to be his wife, and then she was sure of what her answer would be; but these occasions were rare, and it did not oppress her that the question had never come. When the possibility floated across her mind it would not have agreed with her sane, well-regulated nature to let herself go. She was contented with her life as it was. Perhaps also, if she had troubled to look into her own mind closely, she would have found that something else helped her well-regulated nature to remain peaceful—namely, the belief that the question would come. As it was, this conviction existed unacknowledged.

She was sitting in a long wicker chair, with her back half turned to the window which opened on to the verandah. She had a shawl over her shoulders, and say sometimes looking at Henry Bishop standing in front of her, sometimes looking into the room, watching the dust in the sunbeams. Henry stood with his hands behind his back, looking down at the easily reclining figure before him. He appeared almost like an accused before a judge. Not that he was frightened or downcast, but merely that she looked like the person in power, sitting there undisturbed; she might have been holding in her hands the fate of the slightly

bent figure standing before her. The both understood and enjoyed the significance of their relative positions, because they
knew each other well. Certainly he was at a disadvantage, for
she had a right to sit undisturbed. In a sense she had always
been sitting there prepared to acknowledge that her mind was
made up. He, meanwhile, had changed, passed through different phases, approached her, and gone away from her; he had
been tormented, had fallen in love with other people, and finally
found himself actually arriving at a point which he had sometimes before imagined he was nearing. And now she sat listening
to him as he asked her to become his wife. He had been talking
to her of herself, and this was quite new. Until now his conversation had always been of his hopes and fears, and she had
hardly seemed to enter personally into the affair; she had been
sympathetic and convenient. When she felt certain of what he
was saying she let herself go, and acknowledged to herself how
she had thirsted for this speech. She sat perfectly still, smiling,
drinking in his words; now and then she glanced at him, satisfied, feeling that at last it had come, and that she was the pos-
sessor. She did not lose the sense of anything he spoke, and yet
her mind was pleasurably dwelling on the past. His words and
her feelings brought before her mind various times when she
had talked with her; and two stages, two actual occasions, stood
out clearly in the ten years. She had perhaps thought of these
two phases before, but not accurately. Now they came clear and
unmistakable, like two great marks set by fate along the road
which her lover had been ordained to travel...

It was nine o'clock on a September evening eight years before. She and Henry Bishop was sitting on the terrace of the Casino during the interval between the first and second parts of the
ball. Henry had pointed out to her how it always excited him to
come out of a hot, glaring room filled with dancers, and suddenly find himself on the seashore, watching the moon just above
the romantic castle on the cliff, listening to the roll of the pebbles
drawn back b the receding wave. He explained that it was neces-

sary for his appreciation of things that they should move him by
their sensational contrasts. In order to pierce through a dull and
sluggish nature, outside things must be sharp and striking. That
was why he did not care for the country generally. He might look
and look at the trees and fields in spring, but they did not move
him; he could not understand them. But the end of a branch
hanging over the railings of a London square gave him a real
and exciting sensation of spring—and so one. "My life is empty; I have no aim." She felt at that moment that if she gave him
much encouragement he would generously offer her his empty,
aimless life. But she could not. She hardly felt as if it was to her
he was addressing himself more than to any one else. She happened to be there—that was her only qualification. Any other
woman would have done almost as well. Not that what he said
about his empty life was quite false, on the contrary, it was true
to some extent; only it was irrelevant. She had an instinctive feeling that all this was not an integral part of the man's character, it
was merely part of his age. This opinion was so instinctive that
she never formulated it; but she naturally acted upon it. And as
she recalled this evening, other recollections of him came vividly
to mind. His fits of despondency which had no cause, his sudden
transitions to gaiety, the absurd things which he said to her, and
for which he took the trouble to apologise afterwards (the most
ridiculous of all). She had not seen the necessity for this trouble
and searching of heart, and sometimes it fatigued and annoyed
her. When she heard other girls speaking of these romantic ways
of Henry Bishop, whether with praise or censure, she felt that
they were wrong, and that she was right in leaving them alone,
and in perceiving that they were not really Henry Bishop. He
would get out of those ways. Though how this would happen, or
whether she could help him, were questions which would never
have entered her head, even if she had thought carefully and accurately on the subject, which she did not. Indeed, Henry's need
was no imperious. His character was easy, and his nature lightly
composed, so that it did not drag. She remembered, too, a few
occasions when he had confided to her his admiration for other

women. This never made her feel jealous, it was not serious. But it generally wearied her.

Again, it was a chance meeting, four years later, one rainy February morning, in a picture-gallery in Bond Street, three months after the appearance of his paper. He explained his difficulties to her, and he talked of his stories. Again, at this moment, if she had been encouraging, he would have proposed to her. It would have been quite a simple thing—but no, it was impossible. She was not paying very close attention to his account of the plot of the next story. He asked her whether the idea was not a good one, and she answered vaguely, "Yes," and turned her face to look at him. On his features she saw a pained expression: if they had been husband and wife, he would have said to her, "Then you don't take any interest in my life's work? You are not sympathetic? You are not proud being an artist's wife?" No, that she could not have borne. Difficulties she would not have shrunk from; but that kind of difficulty was too much; it was impossible.

But now, now he was standing in front of her, and speaking of himself as loving her personally, loving her passionately. "This is no longer vague romance, this is no longer his work; but it is I, I this actual piece of flesh and blood sitting before him." She did not trouble to interrupt him or to answer him. He needed no answer; but she smiled and kept shifting her eyes from his face to the dusty sunbeam. Fatigue from the dance and the fresh-scented morning air harmonised with her thought, and give her a still and intense joy. It was as if she were in a trance—this lassitude of body, and keenness of mind.

She was looking into the room, her eye was caught by the curtain which had taken the place of the door leaving into the hall. It moved slightly, and

Miss Spencer stood in the doorway. Her aunt was an early riser, and on her way through the hall she had heard a man's voice, so she came to see. Margaret look at her aunt, smiling and undisturbed. If the circumstances had been different she might have felt a little awkward. But now she would not have been disturbed even by a stranger. No, after all these years he was her own, and she would have no interruption. Miss Spencer looked at her niece and saw such an expression of love and satisfaction that she turned and left the room. Henry had never noticed her coming; he stood still in front of Margaret.

· · · · · · ·

Margaret did not tell Helen at once, for now she owed more to Henry than to any one else; but a week afterwards they were talking about it. Margaret was sitting in a great, low chair, and Helen was upon a footstool at her feet.

"We've known each other a very long time, and I'm sure my opinion of him is right: he is settled down now."

Then there was a short pause.

"I suppose there's no man to be found who's really worthy of you, Margaret—"

"Worth? Oh, I don't know, I've simply sat still, I've never done anything. And then worthiness is such a difficult matter to decide. I don't think George is worthy of you in one way; yet I'm sure he's a great artist, and what portion there is of humanity in him is good and attractive."

And as Margaret said the words, Helen looked at her and thought—Then every one is entirely taken up with their own business, and doesn't really care about another's misfortunes or happiness? Margaret, Margaret too has her affairs: each one for himself. "Margaret, who used to be the perpetual sympathiser, is deserting her post, and is going to fight herself now!"

The last sentence Helen spoke aloud, as she turned round and reached her right arm up to encircle her friend's waist, stretching up to her face to touch Margaret's. And then they both cried.

XX.

HELEN came home in August to find George much occupied. He did not wish to go away, for he would only waste his time in the country. He had seen his idol, Mrs. Castellain, a good many times, and had gone to a party at her house where he was rather made the centre of interest. He had thought perhaps Helen and he might go away to the same place as Mrs. Castellain; but when that idea fell through, and she had left town, he could not bear the thought of leaving London and interrupting the work which he had sketched out and shown to her and for which he had won great praise.

All his work had to be connected in his mind with some person. It always had been so. He had attached a corresponding sentiment for some one person to everything which was important or which moved him, even when he was quite a child. It was the same necessity which had made him as a boy think of a lady when he was leaving a place he had lived. The feeling was so subtle, that sometimes it seemed to him as if this need, and the pain at leaving belonged not only to him, but also to her: as if she were wronged by his desertion—a transference of his own feeling to another which made the sentiment doubly penetrating.

When he first saw Mrs. Castellain, she especially asked to be introduced to him. She was a tall, striking woman, exceedingly well dressed. She admired his work, and had wanted to meet him for some time. Helen was introduced, and they went to an evening party at her house in Belgrave Square. She had a grand air, and impressed George as a strict observer of an etiquette with which he was very little acquainted, a fashionable woman who did all the fashionable things, and attached importance to them. There was to George something imposing about her conversation, her occupations, her house, her carriages, her servants; and he was flattered by the attention which she paid him, and the consequence which she attached to him as a rising genius.

Helen did not understand why George found her so imposing—except that she was most striking to look it, and was a beauty of a particular type. And George's tolerance where Mrs. Castellain was concerned simply amazed her. For instance, when she first called on the Aston's, she praised Monty Frere. She had, as a fact, only read Aston's last novel when she met him, and then, too, she had read all the praise, including Frere's. Afterwards she read "Wilmersdorf," without realizing how the book had been blamed.

"Aren't Monty Frere's articles delightful? Especially his weekly page: I've only begun to read them lately."

"Oh, there's no doubt he's a very clever man."

"I always think his criticisms show so much insight, and he's so original, don't you think so?"

"Yes, he certainly gets hold of strong points and puts them well. And he's doing something in literary criticism which no one has done before him."

"In fact, he's one of the new men coming up with new ideas: exactly the critic who is needed for your new movement."

And then she plunged recklessly about George's work, and Helen was quite afraid. But George assented, and was more than diplomatic.

When she had left the house, Helen expressed astonishment at George's tolerance.

"Well, there's no need to go into society with a pen behind one's ear, arguing about theories of art with every one."

"Oh, I think you were admirable." George felt vexed, and answered—

"But what she said was not so devoid of sense either. There was a great deal of truth in it."

In October, "Dieppe" appeared and again divided critics; but the party of admiration was much larger and louder than at the time of "Wilmersdorf."

Mrs. Castellain came back to town; she had seen her husband for a few weeks at Carlsbad. He was an agent for something or other, and was generally in St. Petersburg or Rio, very seldom in London; for when he was free from work he had to go to Carlsbad to get strong again.

George called upon her and gave her a copy of "Dieppe." Mrs. Castellain had seen at once that he was impressed by her pose, and she was flattered, all the more because she knew that she was not really fashionable, and that her distinction was a pretence.

So she was pleased to act the part of initiator to this brilliant young man who was so struck by her; and she drove with him in her carriage, and lent him horses to ride, took him to first nights and introduced him to the few smart people she did know. All the time she had the air of a protector, and he was delighted to join her, and took great care to obey all the little rules which had mad her so admirable in his eyes.

At first Helen was included in her invitations. But naturally she dropped out, for she was not wanted and would not even be impressed. When George began to talk of Mrs. Castellain, she accepted her as the inevitable new idol; but when his admiration for all her ways grew irksome, she said what she thought about her, and wondered how he could be so easily satisfied with a pretentious woman. George grew angry when Helen laughed at her, and so they talked of her no more. And when George did discover that social distinction was rather a thing after which she had always been unsuccessfully striving than a merit already possessed, he only liked her the better; he could feel for her in this, and her need touched the natural kindness of his nature. He joined in her worship of social distinction warmly and sympathetically for her sake.

Some months afterwards, at the beginning of spring, George made another discovery which was most fascinating. He had always been careful to call at the proper hours, and not too often, to behave with a certain stiffness, a kind of good behaviour which was unnatural to him. But he discovered, as he came to know her better, that without making any advances herself, she did not resent little breaches of rules on his part; she never came to meet him, he had to do everything. When he found her show of impassable, irreproachable good breeding was only an exterior, the discovery was wonderful. There she was, passive, tied down by the laws of a game which she had always been trying to play properly, left with little else but immense respect for the laws, and an incapacity to live without them. And George was a source of delight to her the whole time. At the beginning it was pleasure to impress him with her way of life, then it was a new pleasure to go on and play the protector to one who was so easily satisfied, and it was a more intimate pleasure still to feel him shyly and hesitatingly taking liberties, which she herself did nothing.

It was after this discovery of his that Helen began to appear to George rigid and narrow in her frank and upright nature. The feeling came very gradually, and was at first hidden far back in his mind; and besides, he was only doing justice to this other person who had grown so important to him; it would be almost an injury to her not to make some comparison of the kind.

Mrs. Castellain had dark-brown eyes, and fair, very shiny, ashen-yellow hair, which curled upon her forehead. In the evening she wore it in a tapering roll behind, low down upon her neck. And when George came to know her well, he fancied that when they met his sometimes her brown eyes did not look quite straight, as if they showed some internal trouble. Her complexion was perfectly even, without any colour, a thick white, and her lips were hardly less pale than the rest of her face. Often in his boyhood, when he had made new acquaintances, his mother's old friends—the original friends of his childhood—seemed to him mean and small. And just so now he felt towards Helen.

They went away in August to the same place as Mrs. Castellain, and then this new feeling of George's, for until now it had never entered his mind to compare any one with Helen, put something into his manner with her, which made her loneliness more fearful and harassing than when she had spent those miserable weeks in Dieppe three years ago. This admiration was different from any that had gone before, there was something more personal in it which hurt her intimately, the woman seemed really to exert an influence over him. And she herself felt so helpless in a position quite out of character, a position in which all the fine qualities of her nature were useless.

But some months after their return to town, the fear came upon her that George would grow quite apart, irretrievably apart, from her. And she began to think of little things that she had barely noticed before. He went with Mrs. Castellain to theatres and concerts, never with her: he always had time to give to Mrs. Castellain. When George thought of Helen he said to himself, when was perfectly true, that she did not care for entertainments. And if by chance he noticed how perpetually he left her alone, he thought, "It's no pleasure for us to be together, we only irritate each other." And so he shut his eyes and occupied himself with his work and Mrs. Castellain.

Helen could always see in George the man who had given her those gorgeous years, the one great thing in her life, and the sweet companion of two years ago. She spent three months of anguish at the beginning of the year, seeing whether she really was nothing to him. She was infinitely gentle and devoted, and during the short times that she was with him, she spent herself in efforts to gain from him the least sign that she still had a place in his heart. But George did not notice her clearly, he was so deep in his work; his thoughts, too, were full of this other person, and the comparison between the two had grown bolder. As weeks passed on the little things she said to him became shorter and shorter, as if she had hardly breath enough left to say much. Sometimes she would come into the room where he was working, bring him flowers, sit down facing him, and tell him about her walk or about a friend from whom she had received a letter, knowing all the time that the pretty things she said to him were not interesting; yet unable to reach to anything which could touch him, though her heart was breaking. And as she grew more and ore hopeless, she felt as if she were losing all sense, the minute tender speeches which she hardly had the heart to whisper to him seemed to have no meaning as they were spoken. Indeed to George, who was strong and occupied, these little tragic things which she said to him seemed to be fatuous. And she felt that she was losing all her tact, that she was going on when she knew that she was no wanted, as if she were becoming mad.

Then she was seized by a senseless panic fear, she could think of nothing, she had no longer any sense of proportion, terror rushed through her mind, she had no power to stop its course, for there was no actual fear to catch sight of, simply a terrible whirl.

Then came a long period of weariness without any clear thoughts: and then a gradual change into a fixed hopelessness, as if the bitter waters of the last agony had had some hardening, petrifying influence upon her heart.

XXI.

A YEAR passed away. During that time a resolution had formed itself and grown strong inside Helen's mind. Every change that she had gone through, since that visit to Berlin, had come upon her very, very slowly. Each difficulty began by being incomprehensible, and it was only after a long period, occupied by a kind of struggle which was out of her character, that she gradually came to any view of her position. And then, to get over her astonishment and incapacity, and go on from comprehension to forma resolution required another period. Helen was now as slow moving in her own cause as before she had been quick to meet, nay, forestall, any demand upon her sympathy.

She had resolved to leave him. Often before, in the moments of her worst affliction, an unreasoning longing had come upon her to go away, to get away anywhere, away from her surroundings, not with any purpose; simply the desire to go—the desire of all hopeless people. But now this was different; a reasoned, well-considered determination to leave him. And she found some comfort and peace in thinking of this; it would be a certain step, and the only thing left to do. The extreme wild pain which she might have felt did not come upon her: the possibilities of that seemed to have been beaten out of her cruelly and sternly bit by bit. There was only a dull, heavy feeling in her heart when she thought of her departure.

The growth of her resolve and all the accompanying thoughts had been quite her own; she and George had lived so far apart during that time that really she had not considered what he might feel. She would leave him a share of the money—she had arranged all the details in her mind calmly and reasonably. There was no need to wait for any particular opportunity; it was

136

the whole situation which she could not bear. When everything was settled she would tell him. She wondered sometimes how he explained her staying at all, since he showed so little tenderness for her.

One evening in March she determined that the next day she would tell him. She sat in her room soon after breakfast next morning, wondering how she should begin; for though she had thought out again and again what to say, the words of the first sentence had never been decided, and she was angry with herself when she thought that such a thing had to be decided—he was merely to be told. It crossed her mind for an instant that she might say, to begin with, that she was going on a visit, which indeed she might well do. But immediately afterwards she resented the idea. She had come low enough already, bit by bit, in her own estimation; but she would not sink quite to that level of conjugal morality. How terrible it had been, the long struggle which had ruined her high character! How utterly miserable and iron and hopeless and degraded it all was!

As she stood outside his study door, and was going to knock, the picture of herself entering the room flashed before her eyes. For a moment that unnerved her, and she paused. "Why have such things to be explained and done out at length? Why must it all be spoken and acted? Simply the time has come for going, both see it, then they part; but why this actually entering the room, these words?" Then vividly she pictured him sitting inside, wrapped in his work, not dreaming of her, perhaps in his favourite position: the right hand, with the pen in the fingers, on the edge of the table, the other hand touching his left temple, with the elbow resting on the arm of his chair, knowing, as he had explained once, quite well what the next sentence was to be, but purposely not writing it in order to enjoy the feeling of certainty. Or else listlessly idle. He confessed that when he was in difficulties he was generally too lazy to take a piece of paper and write down words as they came into his head, so as to make sure of keeping his attention fixed upon the difficulty, and he was too weak to do something different, go out, talk, or read—he could not help sitting on weakly before his table. Then she thought of Mrs. Castellain—he was not merely a workman, and she knocked.

George had just seen something which illustrated his next point, and to make sure of retaining his vision, he repeated to himself three or four words before he said "Come in." He never minded an interruption when his work was going well, when he saw clearly what was coming next.

Only when she entered the light room, and faced him sitting at his table, did she understand how entirely secret and her own the growth of her resolve had been, and even the thoughts which had swayed her mind long before.

She was struck also by finding him at work. It flashed through her mind that any time would have been a better opportunity. But a feeling that this was false came immediately afterwards. The wish for an opportunity, she knew, was unreasonable; none was needed for what she had to say. For all that, she felt weak; it had seemed simple, and really was simple—just an understanding and it would be over.

"I've come to tell you that I've at last made up my mind—you can't be astonished."

At her appearance and her words George jumped to the conclusion; he thought immediately, though uncertainly—"Mrs. Castellain! she's going to leave me!"

A black general sorrow came upon him, and he stood up from his chair just as she sat down; he could not say "What do you mean?" He could speak nothing but her same—"Helen—"

Suddenly she felt as if something broke, and then the sense of all her wrongs rushed into her mind, the actual ways in which he had wronged her, as she had never seen them before, as if there had been no great difficulty; but simply he had wantonly ill-used her, hit her again and again. Suddenly she was angry, in a passion, at the end of everything, impotent. She hardly recognised herself: there even seemed to be a part of herself remained below the passionate words, looking on.

"It isn't now as it was that other time. You've not only neglected me, made me utterly miserable— treating me all the worse because you won't confess how much you owe to me; but you've insulted me cruelly and at every moment. You are her lover, and her name is on your lips whenever you speak, though you don't say it; her picture is in your eyes whenever you look. And you've done it all gaily, as if it were your right. You've hardly taken the trouble to be ordinarily decent. You allowed me to cringe to you, and you didn't even pretend. It wasn't worth your while to make a show. Why would you? And of course you didn't say, 'Go, I love this other woman, I don't want you,' because you do want me. And what possible excuse is there for you? If she had been a woman with extraordinary qualities, I should have felt that she was more worthy of your love than I. But I haven't even that comfort. You simply were infatuated with her because she was rich; yet you are contented to take from me all your want—It is impossible, impossible!"

And she broke down into passionate crying, all the more wildly because she was coming back from her passion to herself again, with anger against her weakness.

George was not touched as he looked every now and then at the figure of his wife, her hands tightly clasped behind her head, and pulling away from each other, and her eyes fixed in front of her. Only darkness and hopelessness in front of him, with a picture of the other person in the distance, a thing of the past, gone; a thing to be regretted, to be regretted with pain and yearning and anger; but gone. His business was here, with the woman in front of him. He could say nothing except—

"I'm not her lover."

There was a pause. Then her arms fell into her lap.

"Look what you've made of me. Look what I've become. I, Helen Lemardelay, Helen Aston, the woman who was proud, not vainly proud; but because she had high aims, and beliefs that were broader and clearer than those of ordinary people—I've become as small and mean and blind as any one else. Your answer is an answer to my reproach of infidelity! I'm jealous, I've talked of money, I'm brought as low as can be. There have been moments lately when I've thought of proofs, although I've been neglected for years, and my company is plainly no longer anything but a burden. Proofs," she said again to herself, as if she could not measure the depth of her degradation. Then, with utter despair in her voice she went on—

"And nothing can cover that! If the greatest miracle were to happen, it could never touch that; I've thought it, and spoken it, and done it; it's there for ever."

And she slipped down and knelt on the ground with her face buried in her hands on the chair.

So far was George from understanding that he thought her jealousy and sense of injustice quite natural. But thought he did not understand, her words and gestures made him feel the greatness of her agony. He stood silent and hopeless.

Helen stood up from her kneeling position, and put her hand out in front of her, as if to make a division between her passion and what she was going to say now.

"That's all unnecessary, and my fault only."

And sitting down, she went on slowly and softly—

"I've made up my mind to go because it's the only thing left to do. I'm no use here. I've been very, very long finding it out....

I'll only take with me what's necessary, the rest I'll leave with you." She stopped, and her lip quivered, and a mournful smile came into her face as she stretched forward her open right hand upon her knee, deprecatingly, as if to ask for forgiveness—for there was no thought of bitterness in her mind when she said the words. Then she went on speaking.

But George was paying no attention. He had not got beyond the terrible idea of her leaving him. He had kept his eyes willfully closed, going on from day to day, and now at last they had been opened. He felt utterly miserable. There had been little pauses in her speech, but he could not bring himself to say anything: a dull anger at everything prevented any words from coming to his lips. Only it was impossible that they should part.

She got up, and made a movement as if to go. His fear broke upon him decisively, and he came up to her and spoke at last.

"Helen, you can't leave me!" And he went on, without letting her speak. It was his turn to be passionate, to plead despairingly.

"Helen, you mustn't leave me! If you know, you would see how impossible it is. You don't understand how I've gone from day to day without thinking. Can't you forgive me enough to let me try again?"

Helen was astonished; and looking at him she said—

"But you're wrong; I'm sure you're wrong. This is only what you feel at the moment. You are grieved at seeing me like this. I know you're incapable of being unkind when you see me; but it's a mistake to think that it's more than kindness."

"But it's not pity that I feel! It's not at all that."

And truly neither pity nor tenderness for her seemed to him to be in his mind; but only despair that their difference should become hopeless—end in a way which he had never meant and had refused to foresee. What could he say to convince her? He felt as if he were breaking himself against a rock, so just must her resolve seem in her own eyes.

"Don't throw me aside! Don't let it be so utterly hopeless! You can't surely say the final word now? You can't end it all now suddenly and leave me no chance?"

"I must go away; the resolve has grown up so slowly that it is fixed."

"But won't you let me follow you? You must! You haven't the right—surely it's impossible to end everything of your own accord, by yourself, and leave me no hope? And indeed you don't understand—you are wrong. I don't mean about Mrs. Castellain, but altogether. I can say nothing when you tell me how horribly I've wronged you; but it was not intentional—I went on, weakly."

He knew that he could not express himself, for he only felt an incomprehensible despair.

"But it's just your unconsciousness which made it hopeless."

"No; you must believe me in this. Unless you cannot bear me near you, you must believe me and wait and see!"

"I'm so weary!"

"But I won't trouble you. I only want to be there—not out of reach. Tell me that I may stay with you—tell me quickly. Indeed, Helen, I couldn't live on without hope!"

There was such despair in George's voice and look, the agony was so terrifying, that Helen could not refuse him. He might follow her if he wished.

During the rest of the day they spoke little to each other. They were both worn out—weak, so that they could hardly walk.

That night Helen woke up with no memory of her interview with George. She was back with the thoughts of the last months—the resolve to leave him. Her thoughts led her to George, and the last time they had spoken to each other. Then she remembered that he had not left the house that evening, but had gone to his bedroom when she went to hers. Then it came back to her that they were not going to part, and she remembered how the day had been spent. But it seemed to her as if the thoughts with which she had awaked from sleep were really the truth. This new thing could make no difference. Perhaps he would not follow her. Even if he did, what could he do? And she had a dread of beginning the old life over again. She had slowly formed her resolution to go, and now it had come to nothing: she had allowed that they might begin again, although a hundred times she had said to herself that it was impossible. She could not have refused him. But she was going away: that would give her time to think—give them both time. He might not join her; but if he did she could not object. She was troubled by her thoughts; but when she was alone and away from him she would have peace, and time to understand what now only seemed to her confusion—breaking up her resolutions and her views.

XXII.

WHEN Helen started off in the evening of the next day, George could hardly bear to let her go out of his sight. Yet his stay in London after her departure was an arrangement which suited them both. Helen had never foreseen the possibility of such despair as George had shown at the idea of a separation, and even now she could not understand his state of mind. The despair had been most tragically real and earnest; but she still thought at times that it was only for the moment. That was the only way in which she could explain it, and a separation of some weeks might show whether she was right or not. Moreover, even if she were wrong, it would be well not to begin their life again immediately after that interview which had left them both so unnaturally weary, a sudden struggle of strained personal contact after long estrangement.

George had another reason for staying in London. He wished to say good-bye to Mrs. Castellain, and not wrong her by deserting her suddenly and without explanation. As usual, his pain transferred itself largely to her account. It was as if some tormenting spirit, who knew well that man prides himself on his humanity, determined to throw his weight on the wrong side, and suggest to George that he could not comfort himself by saying, "This grief is only my own, and as it affects no on else, I can deal hardly with myself, and not shrink from the pain of breaking with her." But George knew this habit of his so well, that although he was troubled by it as usual, he began to be sceptical.

When he told Mrs. Castellain that Helen had long wanted a change, and had already left London, and that he would follow in two or three weeks, her behaviour did not change in the least. George said nothing pressing enough to make her reveal herself, and he could not tell how much she guessed or what she felt. The two had never talked of Helen, and Mrs. Castellain had put her out of her head, seeing no reason for troubling herself about her, especially as she herself had sat still and every advance in intimacy had come from George. He paid her two visits, and found without intention he had dropped back into the first habit of calling only on her day, when other people were there, and behaving like an admiring stranger. This was exactly the position which he wished to regain: all the same, the change was anguish to him.

His feelings, during the three weeks which he spent after Helen had left, were utterly dreary and black. The prospect of his life with Helen was not a source of cheerfulness. It was a certainty. He had never really wavered; but rejoining her seemed hardly more than a heavy way of continuing life, for what he had said to Helen was true enough—he could not have lived on if parting had been final; and his despair at the idea of breaking with her for ever had been wild as the parting of two lovers through some mistake. Yet at times, when he was less tormented b the painful regret at deserting Mrs. Castellain, and by a general anger against fate because the whole thing had been a mistake, when he got back for a short space to a clearer view, the certainty of his next step was a comfort—not an easy or attractive comfort, but yet well founded. Then for moments he would wonder why he had persisted in begging his wife to let him follow her. Why should he have felt so strongly the impossibility of parting? But he forgot the question in the overwhelming flood of feeling which was always urging him not to lose her. His entire being was for joining her.

He received two letters from Helen, with nothing in them except a few words describing the place in which she was staying. Ever since she had spent a spring in Italy with her mother, when she was fifteen years old, she had wished to go there again. And now in a strange manner the fulfilment of her wish was a distinct pleasure—it was the only thing which found its way into her short letters to her husband. She was staying in the same lodgings as before. The house was kept by an old Scotchwoman, who had been nurse and housekeeper to an English family living in the town. When the family broke up, she had settled in this little house. Helen said that the old woman was delighted to see her again.

As the month drew to a close, George grew more and more impatient to leave London and find himself with Helen. The longer he stayed behind, the more he saw how little there was to be gained by staying, and the more pleasure he took in thinking of his determination to start afresh. It pleased him, because it seemed to show that he was growing older and more able to defend himself against attacks of the moment: though sometimes he shrank from the contemplation, and grew hopeless, and this was when he thought actually of Helen, instead of the whole determination and plan of life apart from detail.

At last he was off, three days sooner than he had intended. He travelled straight on. Every now and then he tried to reason himself out of his excitement at the prospect of seeing Helen; but he only grew more excited as the distance between them lessened.

He had made a mistake about the train; Helen would not be at the station. He left his luggage, and started through the town. He had so little appreciation for anything which was unfamiliar, that he habitually hurried when he was in a strange place. He noticed the square white houses in the important streets, and the look of the black print on the white walls, the peculiar shape of the letters at street corners. He now and then asked the way, simply speaking the address, and he was shown the road which he felt would have taken of his own accord. At the end of the town the street went up hill, a kind of faubourg, with fine villas on each side, and after the last houses there came a wood. The road mounted straight up—one of those roads which inevitably lead up to a view of the sea— and Helen lived on the other side.

George could hardly help running to get over the last twenty yards to the top. Then he saw a square piece of the sea at the bottom of the road, very blue, cut off by the trees which grew thickly on either side. He walked more slowly down hill. When he came to the bottom, he found that he was still some distance from the sea, and the road turned and ran straight for about half a mile to a small cluster of houses. He walked on, still trying not to be excited. The house where Helen was staying was called Paisley Lodge, and he found it just in the natural place. He went up to it, his hand trembling and his heart beating; then he crossed the threshold, and saw Helen's ulster hanging up, and her umbrella in the corner. He pushed open the door of the sitting-room on his left hand, and there was Helen's writing-case on the table, and other things of hers met his eye at once, and moved him so that he could have shouted. It seemed as if there was such an air of Helen in the room, that he would have recognised it as hers without the help of these objects which he knew. Helen had evidently gone out; it was still early in the morning—only half-past nine. George turned to follow her, as if he knew which way she had gone. A little Italian servant-girl, coming in at the door, met him, and called at once for Mrs. Gutherie, who appeared from the back of the house. George was glad when he saw the Scotchwoman.

"Mrs. Aston—Miss Lemardelay, as I knew her, she added—"is gone out, sir. She did not expect you till this evening."

"No; I made a mistake when I wrote. I'll go out and find her."

Mrs. Gutherie went with him into the road, and pointed in the direction which Helen had taken. It was up the road down from which he'd come.

"You will see a path, sir, on your left hand, when you are half-way up among the trees. I think she went there, for I know it's a favourite place of hers."

George walked up the hill, noticing each thing more close-ly as he passed. He found the path leading off the road, and went into the wood out of the sun. He walked slowly and softly among the trees. If he had been sure Helen was not there, he would have called out her name; but he stopped his mouth and crept about slowly, knowing that at any turn he might see her. And there she was! On his left there was a break in the wood and a view over the sea, and she was sitting in the shade of a tree, on the grass among the anemones.

She saw him almost at once, and she held out her right hand without moving from her position, looking at him with a smile on her face, until he reached her; then she dropped her hand upon the grass, and he lay down by her side. As soon as he was there looking at her, directly she spoke, the romance of that morning had gone. There was once more only the difficulty.

"You've found me out."

"Yes; more by instinct, it seems to me, than by the directions I was given."

"So you came all the way without stopping?" "Yes. I made a mistake about the train; I thought it came in twelve hours later than it really did."

And except what Helen told him of the places which she had visited during her stay, that was all the conversation they ever had about the past.

For the first two or three days they went about behaving like children who have both been punished for some common mis-deed; drawn more closely together by the punishment, yet not sympathetic and warm, because they fear is still upon them, and they cannot speak of it to each other.

The difficulty had never been out of Helen's mind, and im-mediately George joined her it became menacing. But after she had gone through the first day, she determined that she would not be oppressed by it. During the month which she had spent alone, she had tried to collect herself. Perhaps he would not come; at any rate, she would expect nothing, ask nothing. She would try and break herself of that entire dependence upon their common life, which had brought her only disappointment, and left her with no life of her own. She would be easier; not that she would draw back now, or put any difficulties in George's way—she was incapable of attempting such a thing—but she was determined to try, at all events, to be less intensely harassed by the want of sympathy which she would feel. But just this behaviour in Helen troubled George. Often during the first few days, after they had been out for a walk, talking disjointedly just about occurrences of the moment, both a little tired and at a loss, she wished that Helen would come to meet him, show a keener need for his company, be less unattached and indisposed to make demands on upon him. As it was, he had to strengthen himself coldly by remembering how firmly he had resolved to make up for his past neglect of Helen, and such conscientious, inhuman dealing was out of character. Something he wanted to come from her which would make his part easier, some warmth and sympathy which would remove the difficulty and bring them close together. But they had travelled on diverging roads for so many years, and there was no point of contact to be found in the past.

When they first fell in love with each other, they had needed nothing to bring them together, and Helen wondered why they could find no true intimacy now, why she felt constrained and tired, and sometimes anxious now that she was with him all day long. She felt uncomfortable that he should always be at her service, that he should have no occupation but to be with her. That which had been natural in the first days of their love seemed abnormal now.

One evening they both sat down at the table to write letters. George finished his, and, after sitting still a few minutes, he went out of the room and came back with a packet of papers in his hand. The shape was familiar to Helen; he always wrote on the same paper, folded the same way. She had a sudden feeling of relief. While writing her third letter, she watched him. He read the first two or three pages very carefully, then the following pages more and more quickly, and at last he only turned them over, till he reached the place where the writing stopped; and then he turned back and read some few pages before; and then he looked at the loose sheets, which he had put beside him when he sat down, on which she could see scribbled notes. Her heart grew lighter as she looked at him. She thought of the three stories which he had published since his "Dieppe." She had liked one better than the other. The last, "A Lady Novelist," she remembered especially; it had appeared four months ago, and she thought it magnificent. She read it in the midst of her sorrow, and its very magnificence seemed to make her own life only more hopeless. She wrote a fourth letter—she felt an inclination to talk to her friends—she could have written endless letters.

The evening wore on; their eyes seldom met; George only saw that she was always writing a letter.

At last she laid down her pen, and looked fixedly at George. He was writing, but was sitting still with his head on his hand. Suddenly he laughed, half to himself, without opening his mouth, as a man laughs over a book when some one else is in the room. An impulse came upon her; she laughed too, aloud. He looked up astonished; and she was kneeling at his side, with her right hand on his, and her left stretching up to his shoulder. She said eagerly—

"Do you think it can be better than 'A Lady Novelist?'"

.   .   .   .   .   .

"But I won't be extravagant in my hopes," she said to herself when she was alone. "I will let things take their course." And she wondered over the trouble of the last six years. How had it come

about! What had she been struggling for? And was outside opinion, after all, the source of the whole difficulty? If her husband's
work was not disgraceful in the eyes of the world, if it won him
praise and honour, was that all a woman thought of? But she
would not puzzle over the past.

"I have grown older" she thought, and with those words in
her head she fell asleep.

XXIII.

YEARS passed away. Helen and George travelled about, sometimes staying in London for a few months, but with no fixed home. They settled down at last in London, and in Kensington. The High Street had changed a great deal, there was no sign left of the Lemardelay's old house; but Kensington Square, except for one or two red-brick buildings, which to George's disgust had taken the place of the simple old houses, was the same, and there they lived.

George's writing had gone on steadily. He had long passed the stage of development when he had needed a sympathetic listener for his theories: he had become a regular workman. And he might be idle for as many weeks as he liked; no one would have dreamed of questioning his right, for he was a great novelist. His first volume of stories was republished. He made a few alterations here and there, chiefly omissions, but he saw very little that wanted changing, they seemed to him astonishingly good. Some had forgotten and some had never known the adverse criticism which the book had roused, and everybody admired it. Many of his most distinctive good qualities came out in these stories. He himself was pleased and astonished to see how fearless he had been, unconsciously putting down exactly what he meant as well as he could, without any thought of what people would say.

He knew that he had a fund of material still to be used; but it was comforting to feel that he had the right to look back and say to himself that even if he wrote no more he had done enough. Overwhelming success had taken the difficulties from his life and left it narrow and calm, and he was free to look at his wife and honour her for her strength. And Helen was filled with endless admiration for his work and pride in his success, finding life easy and occupation everywhere, knowing too, when girls came to her with their insatiable thirst for the most subtle, untiring sympathy, that there was something else in life which they did not understand—a still contentment, a feeling of satisfaction that the road lies straight and clear before the eyes.

There was only one thing in George's life besides his work— his relation to Helen, their capacity for living together, which at the end of all trials had come out a sure fact. And as this was so, Helen was satisfied to see George gradually win for himself the sublime right of treating everything outside his work and his relation to her as if it had been part of some extravagant bur- lesque in which he happened to be acting.

The set of more or less distinguished men and women to which the Astons belonged was collected together as usual one evening at the house of a successful portrait painter, Ramsay. His friends had been laughingly asking Aston which side he took in a newspaper discussion about some point in his work.

"Why couldn't it all have come sooner?" he complained. "Why couldn't I have had my portrait in the papers and been boomed when I was still young and sentimental enough to want to make personal capital out of my fame? Who cares now? My work, of course, is always there, a pleasure in itself, and outside praise doesn't add very much to the pleasure; but why couldn't I have been famous when it would have been a joy for me to walk with a halo round my head? I had dreams when I was a boy of marching through the streets at the head of conquering troops— heaven knows what troops!—but troops, with everybody shouting, and ladies waving handkerchiefs from the balconies. Why couldn't I have had my conquering troops up the High Street then, when I should have enjoyed the balco- nies, instead of having my portrait and a sketch of my life, and correspondence about the moral teaching in the characters of my women, in the papers now, when my time is spent between my own room, and the close circle of my intimate friends?"

When the jokes and comments upon his complaint had subsided, Mrs. Ramsay said—

"Well, Mr. Aston, at the school which my niece has just left, there was a society called the 'Astonians'—of course you've never heard of them. Margery was made the high-priestess because she was the only one who had ever been in the same room with you, moreover, she had stolen my copy of 'Love's Highway' with your autograph in it. They all used to have photographs of you pinned inside their desks. I must introduce you to Margery; for complete adoration..."

A fortnight later the girl was introduced to her idol. When the visit was over, Margery was angry with herself because she had said nothing. She had taken off her glove to shake hands with him, and she had brought him his cup, though she trembled so much that she had to hold it with both hands, and then she had to sit silent, hardly daring to look at him. He was not quite as she had expected; but, of course, he was perfect as he was. She had thought his hair was quite black, and that he was younger looking, and yet when she met him she recognised the man who she had seen two years before. In between, rather a different idea of him had grown up; but that was quite a schoolgirl's romance, and she was ashamed of herself. It was much better that his dark hair should be turning grey, and that there should be deep lines on his face, marks set by sorrow, and fierce passions lived through. Yes, he was perfect as he was. And he had asked her to come with her aunt and see him.

Soon afterwards she went to see him in his own house, she even went into his study. She had fancied a room curiously and richly furnished, filled with wonderful books, and she found a big, bare room, with no carpet, a large writing-table with a few papers on it, two or three chairs, a second table, and on the walls some drawings, and a row of books, chiefly in paper covers. She again felt ashamed of her school-girl ideas. She could not help being surprised, too, that a man whose novels were so serious and passionate should talk of everything in such a light, amused fashion. Helen she thought simply divine, she had always heard her admired, and her expectations were not disappointed: she stood such a fine figure beside her husband; indeed, she must be a marvellous woman to be the companion of such a man.

She could not help wondering whether she had made any effect on him, though she was horrified at her audacity in thinking of such a thing: simply to see him was all she could wish for—and to shake hands!... She imagined that he had noticed her, that he was pleased to talk to her, and had found her pretty. It was wonderful; she longed to let everyone know that she had visited him in his house. Perhaps at some party (she was just coming out), where there were crowds of people, he would come and talk to her!

One afternoon, a few days later, Mr. and Mrs. Aston were calling on Mrs. Ramsay. No one else was in the room except the lady of the house and Margery. The girl was marvelling at heaven's peculiar flavour; she was allowed to see the great man so close, she was treated as if she had a perfect right to be one of such a party, one of four friends sitting and chatting. She had said very little, but soon the conversation turned upon her, and George said he remembered quite well seeing her there two years before—

"Only then you had your hair down. You don't mind my reminding you of this? It isn't so bad as when your friends remarked how you'd grown, is it? Of course it's very wonderful to put your hair up; but don't girls ever remember how pretty they looked when it was down?"

"Shall I let it down for you?" Margery said, smiling and her cheeks—and her hat was on her lap with pins in it, and her hands up to her head, and in a second her hair came tumbling wavy and golden over her shoulders.

"Yes, that's how you looked. How charming of you to let your curls rest as they used to."

For a moment Margery had felt terribly afraid at her boldness as she sat looking at Aston; but his words and his smile put her directly at her ease, and everybody talked and laughed so prettily afterwards that she became intensely happy; and when the Astons left, Helen kissed her. Margery could not express her gratitude to her aunt, she had never spent such a gorgeous afternoon.

They met frequently, and George transported her to heaven by always speaking to her and making much of her. He even wrote a preface to some of her poems and had them published. On the appearance of the volume a critic remarked that all great writers, when they grew old, had taken to protecting impossible young verse-makers; the signs of old age had come unexpectedly upon Aston. One of his friends asked him what possessed him to introduce such drivel into the world.

"If a line of it isn't meaninglessly commonplace, the reason simply is that this silly school-girl hasn't been able to reach her usual level."

"Of course they're commonplace, that's just what's so delicious about them. It's delightful to think of this sweet child sitting down, dipping her pen in the ink, and writing these verses—how extraordinarily dull and stupid people are!"

When the summer holidays came, Margery had to go to some German baths with her family. She was in despair at the thought of missing George's society. She could not conceive how it was that people were allowed to take away from her the whole joy of her life like that, for two months. No one could comfort her.

George received a long letter from her, written the day she left. He answered it and then he heard no more from her.

At the end of September Helen told George that she had just received a note from Mrs. Ramsay, saying that her niece was engaged to be married. At

Kissingen they had made the acquaintance of a young fellow, Vincent Dalgleish, who had just left Sandhurst, and after a little more than a month they were engaged. Everybody had been very much shocked, and Mrs. Poole declared she would not consider it a formal engagement. The young man excused himself by saying that he had to go to Ireland, and he wanted to make sure first.

"Well, these young people are sudden. I hope he's a good fellow—but why didn't she write and tell us all about it?"

He sat silent for a moment, and then broke out laughing—

"I know why she didn't write! She was shy because she'd thrown me over! Really these girls are charming. She has found the genuine article now! She isn't much like the rest of her family, is she?"

"A little like Mrs. Ramsay; don't you think so?"

"Yes, perhaps she is. Of course the Ramsays are coming to dinner this evening, aren't they? And who else is coming?"

ABOUT ODD VOLUMES

The publishing imprint of The Fortnightly Review is named after The Sette of Odd Volumes, a private dining club of biblio-philes, publishers, writers, illustrators and artists, bookbinders, editors, scholars, and eccentrics founded in 1878 by the celebrat-ed antiquarian bookseller Bernard Quaritch (23 April 1819—17 December 1899). The society's monthly meetings were aimed at bringing together all the members, each of whom had a desig-nated expertise, to create a perfect "sette of odd volumes." The society published a very long list of "opuscala"—small, hand-made chapbooks on a wide variety of topics to accompany the talks given by members. An archive is at Cambridge University.

For our current O.V. catalogue, visit

http://fortnightlyreview.co.uk/odd-volumes/

www.ingramcontent.com/pod-product-compliance
Lightning Source LLC
Chambersburg PA
CBHW060224180626
46813CB00007B/2948